A SLIGHT MISUNDERSTANDING

Mary's very nearness was driving the duke to distraction. He wanted to touch her, to crush her curls in his fingers, to bring her lips up to his, to have her in his complete possession. The housemaid with the dark violet eyes favored the duke with a blushing smile so lovely that his heart began to race, and then, she spoke.

"It is so very hard to believe, Charles. Are you really offering me the protection of your name?" said Mary, looking up at the Duke of Sarratt with tears in her eyes, tears of happiness, love, and trust.

"My name?" said the duke, suddenly confused.

"Yes. Yes, of course. You are offering to marry me, sir, are you not?"

"I was offering to *keep you under my protection*," said his grace firmly, speaking in a clipped, formal tone meant to disabuse the silly chit of any more such awkward, irritating notions. "I am asking you to become my mistress!"

She had slapped him full across the face before she knew what she was doing, crying out, "How *dare* you!"

The sheer insolence of the man! How *could* he have asked her to be his doxy, his ladybird, his Cyprian? She had never been so angry with anyone. She would have killed him in an instant, given the chance!

ZEBRA REGENCIES
ARE THE
TALK OF THE TON!

A REFORMED RAKE   (4499, $3.99)

by Jeanne Savery

After governess Harriet Cole helped her young charge flee to France—
and the designs of a despicable suitor, more trouble soon arrived in the
person of a London rake. Sir Frederick Carrington insisted on providing
safe escort back to England. Harriet deemed Carrington more dangerous than any band of brigands, but secretly relished matching wits with
him. But after being taken in his arms for a tender kiss, she found
herself wondering—*could* a lady find love with an irresistible rogue?

A SCANDALOUS PROPOSAL   (4504, $4.99)

by Teresa DesJardien

After only two weeks into the London season, Lady Pamela Premington
has already received her first offer of marriage. If only it hadn't come
from the *ton's* most notorious rake, Lord Marchmont. Pamela had already set her sights on the distinguished Lieutenant Penford, who had
the heroism and honor that made him the ideal match. Now she had to
keep from falling under the spell of the seductive Lord so she could
pursue the man more worthy of her love. Or was he?

A LADY'S CHAMPION   (4535, $3.99)

by Janice Bennett

Miss Daphne, art mistress of the Selwood Academy for Young Ladies,
greeted the notion of ghosts haunting the academy with skepticism.
However, to avoid rumors frightening off students, she found herself
turning to Mr. Adrian Carstairs, sent by her uncle to be her "protector"
against the "ghosts." Although, Daphne would accept no interference
in her life, she *would* accept aid in exposing any spectral spirits. What
she never expected was for Adrian to expose the secret wishes of her
hidden heart . . .

CHARITY'S GAMBIT   (4537, $3.99)

by Marcy Stewart

Charity Abercrombie reluctantly embarks on a London season in hopes
of making a suitable match. However she cannot forget the mysterious
Dominic Castille—and the kiss they shared—when he fell from a tree
as she strolled through the woods. Charity does not know that the dark
and dashing captain harbors a dangerous secret that will ensnare them
both in its web—leaving Charity to risk certain ruin and losing the man
she so passionately loves . . .

Available wherever paperbacks are sold, or order direct from the
Publisher. Send cover price plus 50¢ per copy for mailing and
handling to Penguin USA, P.O. Box 999, c/o Dept. 17109,
Bergenfield, NJ 07621. Residents of New York and Tennessee
must include sales tax. DO NOT SEND CASH.

False Pretenses
Isobel Linton

ZEBRA BOOKS
KENSINGTON PUBLISHING CORP.

ZEBRA BOOKS are published by

Kensington Publishing Corp.
850 Third Avenue
New York, NY 10022

First Printing: January, 1996

Printed in the United States of America

Chapter 1

"I don't care a fig which well-bred chit you marry, Charles, but marry you must and marry you shall!" declared the small, silver-haired noblewoman, setting down her delicate bone-china teacup with an alarming zeal. "After all, you have a duty to continue your name and lineage."

Charles Wellesford, 6th Duke of Sarratt, could hardly disagree with this last point. He allowed himself to sigh, briefly. What was a duke to do? Moved to a thoughtful silence, his grace polished his quizzing-glass with a fine linen handkerchief as he contemplated a suitable reply to his beleaguered parent's imperative.

He sympathized with her feelings, truly he did, but he was most unwilling to oblige her grace in this matter, however loudly duty called. The handsome Duke of Sarratt felt himself, for all his high position, rather like a prisoner at Newgate—one already sentenced to the gallows, and merely awaiting the summons to meet his doom. That summons, it seemed, had finally arrived today; for a true nobleman, there remained only the obligation to display a final show of bravery in the face of apparently inevitable ill fate.

Truth be told, the duke had always profoundly wished he might never have to be so tested. Marriage was, all things considered, a revolting thought, and, as if to demonstrate this, a great shudder shook his broad shoulders as the thought of actually having to take a *wife* arose most vividly in his mind.

The idea of becoming leg-shackled had always been abhorrent to him, and even now, when the question of the succession undoubtedly required settlement once and for all, he remained unwilling to coerce himself into taking that final, dreadful, irrevocable step. The duke of Sarratt rose and took a brisk turn around his mother's gilded sitting-room, while his mind worked to put together a strategy to deal deftly with the desperate threat that had been presented to him.

At thirty-four, the duke of Sarratt was an excellent figure of a man, powerfully built, and with a natural strength that had been honed by regular sparring at Jackson's Rooms on Bond Street. Gentleman Jackson himself proudly counted his grace as one of his most talented students. Sarratt was a notable whip, and drove to an inch, though he had never wished to advertise the fact, as he called it, by joining the Four in Hand Club. He was known to all as an excellent judge of horseflesh; a bruising rider, he kept no pack of his own, as well he might have had he so desired, but spent much of his time in the country at his hunting box, riding to hounds with the Melton. His grace was a perfect Corinthian—very much a man's man, which is perhaps why this conversation with his mother, upon a topic which was of most concern to the opposite sex, left him so uneasy.

In the end, the Duke of Sarratt decided to temporize,

a tactic he had employed with obvious success all these sixteen gloriously untrammeled happy bachelor years. There had to be a way out. Surely he could find a way to buy himself more time.

"Most certainly I shall marry, Mother," was his grace's reply at last, delivered with the duke's customary evenness. "I promise you I shall."

"But when, Charles?" said the dowager, suspicious of her beloved only son, and not without reason.

"Soon, Mama. Very soon."

"And for whom will you offer?" added her grace. "I own I am curious to know who you consider worthy to make the next duchess of Sarratt."

"Adelaide? Caroline? Arabella?"

"Charles!"

"I don't believe I care a fig which chit I marry, either, Mama, so it really matters not. There are so many of them, so very many. How can one make any distinction? I assure you, I cannot. All those husband-hungry girls at Almack's, standing around simpering in their costly laces and paint, gabbling like famished geese—in truth, I dislike them all cordially. What choice is there in that? Any of the female sex will suffice me as a wife." His dark brown eyes held within them a masked and dangerous gleam as he added, "That being the case, and there being so very many candidates, any time would serve to do the deed, would it not?"

The Duke of Sarratt waited a moment before he added, gingerly, hoping in this quiet way to manage a reprieve, "But not just *yet,* I think."

The dowager duchess studied her son with concern and incomprehension, drinking her tea reflectively, then carefully setting her china cup into its saucer with a decided snap. Her still-fair cheeks flushed lightly pink with exasperation.

"Not yet? Not *yet*, Charles? A score of years in which to choose a wife has proved insufficient for you! No, no, no, I love you dearly, but I have had enough of your sweet words and sweeter mad reasonings. No, it cannot go on this way, my dear. I will not allow it. You must offer for some female. You cannot keep procrastinating and putting the matter off any longer. It will not do!"

"Won't it do, dear, really?" said the duke, taking his mother's hand in his, and flashing her his most endearing smile. "Are you quite, quite sure?"

The Dowager Duchess of Sarratt looked at her son sadly, and with great love. She devoutly wished her husband were still alive to give his son some guidance; she wished that Charles had not succeeded to his high title at such a young age, for it was that, perhaps, that had hardened his disposition and made him so cynical of the ambitious marital intentions of the fair sex.

"I am sorry, dearest Charles, but, no, it will not do. I am old, now. I do not have many years remaining. More than anything else, I would like my old age to be ameliorated by a warm acquaintance with some grandchildren. More than anything else, I would like the opportunity to hold your own son and heir in my arms, or to help raise your daughter. Can you not oblige me in this?"

"Are we *sure* there is no other solution to the dilemma? Perhaps . . . I might try to adopt?" he asked, with a desperate humor. His mother shook her head, unamused, and the duke, feeling rather guilty, continued.

"It has always been my wish to serve you, Mama. However, I feel sure you are aware of my problem—you can hardly have failed to notice that I am constitutionally unable to care for any woman. Surely you of all persons are aware that there has never been any woman in my life; there has never been any woman that I have ever loved other than you. Particularly in my youth, I attended all the proper balls and assemblies, making myself available to encounter a mate. That did not come to pass, however, even over a series of seasons so long I cannot count them."

"You never tried, Charles. Not really."

"I have tried, Mama. I have tried to care for other women, and I have failed, always, utterly. Other than you, and sometimes Diana, when she's not in one of her sulky moods, I simply don't enjoy the company of women. Look at me, Mother. Would you truly have me marry just to breed?"

There was a moment of silence.

"At this point, I do believe I would."

This provoked a loud peal of laughter from his grace.

"You've bested me all my life, you know, Mother. I feel that I am vanquished now."

The dowager then replied, with perfect seriousness, "Charles, I would have you happy in your marriage, just as I was. You must know that."

"Were you happy, truly?"

"Yes, I was. As should you be."

"You must see that that outcome, desirable though it would be, is long past hoping for."

"I am sorry for that, my son. The fact remains, nonetheless, that marriage is expected of you. *I* expect it of you."

The duke answered his mother in a dark and sober tone, as would a general handing over his sword, surrendering his army to the enemy after a last, long, hard-fought battle.

"Very well, then, Mama. If it must be so, then I am resigned to it, and I shall do just that! I am reluctant to do it; more than that, I am appalled. In fact, not to put too fine an edge on it, the thought of marriage fills me with horror—"

"Charles, no!"

"But if it is your earnest wish, then I am resigned to it, and I shall wed. I give you my word I shall wed—soon."

He let a sigh escape his lips. "I shall do it only to please you, and only to give you the grandchildren you desire."

The dowager duchess considered this. She nibbled at a particularly delectable raspberry tart, dusted the crumbs from her bejeweled hands, and then shook her head in ever-heightening disbelief.

"I cannot pretend to understand your attitude, Charles. How can you be so cold-blooded about it? I do not believe you to be a man entirely lacking in passion and sensibility—after all, at least in your first youth, you kept a mistress."

"In my youth, I behaved as many young, foolish men do, and spent a large amount of money and precious time on the shallow, useless, impermanent pleasures afforded by an empty-headed Cyprian. I do think it is rather indelicate of you to mention that, Mama."

"Rubbish! Don't be such a prig! In my day we did not display such sensibility about these perfectly ordinary things. Fancy pieces are a part of life . . . they were certainly part of your father's life."

"Yes, madam, I was always well aware of *that,*" replied Sarratt, with an uncharacteristic bitterness his mother failed to note. "I had hoped not to emulate him in that respect."

"Then you have succeeded. You must have had, at some time in your life, successful dealings with young ladies of the opposite sex. You must have had some, how shall I say? Some . . . well, some *feelings* for them. You must find some of the many young ladies of the ton, so to speak . . . *attractive* to you. Do you not ever feel some . . . attraction toward them?"

The duke leaned toward his mother, as if to emphasize his explanation.

"That is just the point I have been trying to make: I'm afraid I do not have, as you so delicately put it, any *feelings* for them. No, excepting yourself, I do not like women. I do not like the whole sex. After the first rush of youth, I grew tired of my Cyprian, and tired of all the many well-bred young ladies of my acquaintance. In my opinion, they are, one and all, frivolous, ignorant, spiteful, self-absorbed, simpering, selfish misses. And I have no use for them, Mother. If they were like you—anything like you—I should feel differently. But they are not— and that's the end of it."

The dowager duchess shook her head, wondering where this all would lead. Finally, she said, impulsively, "Oh, Charles. I do feel sorry for you."

A tall, dark man of exquisite aspect in manners as in dress, the duke rose and walked the few steps to the chair where his mother was sitting. He took her hand in his and pressed it in his with great affection. Then he let the small hand go, leaned over, and gently kissed his mother on the cheek.

"Don't feel sorry for me, Mama. I love you, and I love you dearly, but as to the rest of it, it's hopeless—I am what I am. From the bottom of my heart, I do not wish to marry—not anyone, not at any time. That is my nature."

His grace sighed and walked to the opposite side of the room. He noted with approval that his ward had done an excellent job of arranging flowers for his mother's room, realizing that while his ward Diana had been presented and was out in society, she had not "taken," and the critical business of making a match for *her* must be seen to. All things considered, it would be much easier for the girl if she were taken under the wing of his own wife and shepherded by her through the rest of the season.

The dowager had grown far too frail to withstand the assault of a whole year of husband-hunting at Almack's, and he himself had no stomach for such female things.

Logically, it was the thing to do. No coward in defeat, Sarratt looked out the long window for a moment onto Park Lane as if bidding a final good-bye to his freedom, and then turned back to his mother again, saying, "However, mindful of my duty to my family, I am fully prepared to resign myself to entering into a marriage of convenience."

"It is not what I would have wanted for you, my dear."

"But it is the best that can be. Don't regard it, I beg you. If I am to be compelled by circumstance to do this—and I realize that I must—I will choose myself a female. I will wed her."

"Oh, very well, then."

The duke's voice was marked by an odd tightness as he added, "I—I can think of several candidates of excellent breeding whom I am sure you will find unexceptionable, Adelaide Henchart and Caroline Morton first among them. How I personally feel about the chits is of no consequence."

His mother, appalled, made no reply. How she wished she could find some girl for him to love—a female not just in the common way, but a girl of excellent character, one who would know and love her son for what was best in him, and could bear with his shortcomings and seek to lessen them through her very presence. Someone who could be of help to poor Diana, who seemed to be having difficulty finding her place in society, and someone who could be a consolation to herself in her old age.

"I shall accede to your wishes, Mama. I simply must screw my courage to the sticking place and make a final choice. Adelaide or Caroline. Sarah, Anthea? Oh, dash it all—which one of those dreary lovelies shall it be?"

Her grace listened well to her son's words. Unable to reply at once, she paused for some moments, contemplatively. A stray silver-white curl escaped the confines of a French lace cap and slipped down onto her forehead. She was perplexed, and more than a little disheartened that in the end, this scene was occurring.

The dowager duchess of Sarratt looked at her only child and tried to consider her son dispassionately. He was an intelligent, handsome, daring, darling creature, a Pink of the Ton, a Corinthian, a nonesuch—but for all these virtues, the duke seemed to have been born without a heart.

To her, he was a loving son, and to his desperately shy young ward, the Honorable Diana Leigh, he was a fond and firm guardian—but beyond the females of his own family, it seemed he had never encountered a woman who had engaged his affections. Worse yet, it increasingly seemed as if Charles actually did not desire to *have* his affections engaged. Even the light-skirts of his youth had been discovered and discarded within a month at most. And now he claims to cordially dislike the entire female sex! The dowager duchess found it all most disconcerting.

Her grace raised her blue eyes to him, and stated in what she devoutly hoped was a neutral tone, ''Either Lady Adelaide Henchart or Caroline Morton would suffice, I suppose.''

Sarratt's lips pursed into a line. His grace paused carefully before giving his answer, flipping open an enamel snuffbox and taking a pinch.

''Yes, I suppose it must be one or the other. All things considered, I think that Lady Adelaide is my choice for my duchess. She is somewhat less stupid than Caroline, though more irritating. Sarah Simmons is too young and too temperamental. Lady Anthea Pattison, though a wealthy, sportive, and rather amiable chit, has the face of a walrus, and the manners of an ostler. I couldn't bear to live with such a one—the bedroom would end up smelling like the stables."

"Charles!"

"All right, then. Adelaide must head the list. I shall begin to pay her court."

His mother sighed, and tried to find properly diplomatic words in which to express her opinion. She took a final sip of tea, and paused before she spoke.

"Charles, I must say that, though the girl *is* well enough born, and though she would certainly be better than your taking no wife at all, I'm not sure I'm terribly—how shall I put it?—comfortable with the idea of having Adelaide as my daughter-in-law."

"Indeed? Then you can perhaps appreciate how *I* feel at the thought of taking her to wife," said his grace dryly.

"Charles," said her grace with a warning look.

"Forgive me. Surely you must see that the whole idea of marriage is disastrous for me, no matter which wife I might take," replied the duke. "In your perfection, you have spoiled me for all other women."

"Stop your flattery! Make no more excuses, Charles. Marry!"

"Comes to mind the advice of the Apostle Paul. I wonder about it—*is* it better to marry, or to burn?"

"To marry!"

Said her son, in the driest tones imaginable, "Well, *I'd* sooner burn."

At this, the dowager duchess of Sarratt broke out into uncontrollable whoops of laughter. "Charles, what am I to do with you? Sometimes I think I do not know you at all. You are quite impossible! You must marry!"

"Marry—anyone but Adelaide?"

"Beastly child! Go ahead and marry Adelaide! I'm sure that if you can stomach her, I can!"

"Oh, no, Mama—it won't do. You cannot have things both ways. You said only minutes ago that it doesn't matter to you which one of these girls I choose to marry, so long as I do marry one of them. As you have said, let it be so, and mind that you keep your word! If you want me to marry, you mustn't cavil at my choice. Even if it is," and here her grace winced gently, "Lady Adelaide Henchart."

The duchess was hard pressed to keep her temper in check, but her many years of profound training in deportment served her well. She allowed her son to continue.

"As it happens, Mama, Lady Adelaide has rather a large advantage over the rest of my bevy of would-be duchesses. Being of noble birth, very nicely brought up, Adelaide is fully prepared to understand and accept that if she were to become my wife, we two would lead separate lives; she would be, I think, perfectly prepared to promise not to interfere with me in any way. She would be a conformable spouse, well satisfied not to bother me, but just to enjoy the benefits of my rank and my fortune."

"As would any woman."

"Not all women would be satisfied not to sit in my pocket, I think, though probably any woman would enjoy becoming a wealthy duchess. Adelaide would realize that it is a reasonable thing that there should be some price to pay for becoming the Duchess of Sarratt—and that price is simply to leave her husband be!

"You see, that is all that I require in my future wife— that she leave me alone."

"My poor Charles—have I brought you up so lovelessly, so wrongly?"

"Not at all, my dear. It's just that, as I've said, no one else can compete with you. You've spoiled me for any other woman."

"What a shameless flatterer you are, Charles," said

her grace, her eyes filled with love and undisguised compassion for her cold-hearted child, as the duke kissed her hand and bowed himself out of the room.

When he had gone, she twisted the heirloom rings on her fingers, shaking her head and wondering what would ever become of her very darling, but very stubborn and hard-to-please son. It might almost be worth trying to arrange for him to marry his own ward, Diana Leigh, after she came of age, for Diana was a conformable girl. Diana, however, was years away from her majority, and it would not do at all for a ward to marry one who was still her legal guardian. No, that marriage would be too many years away; and the duchess longed to have grandchildren to spoil and to dandle on her knee. Charles would just have to marry someone else, and do so quickly. The duchess vowed that she would live to see her grandchildren, and that it would happen this very year—even if, in order to achieve her fondest wish, she *did* have to bear with Lady Adelaide Henchart as her daughter-in-law.

Chapter 2

"Charles! You old devil! Where have you been? I've seen a pair of bays at Tatt's that I must have your opinion on! Sit down and I'll tell you all about them! You, too, Fitz—come here and pull up a chair, it's all over: Sarratt come by to settle it all for us!"

Lord Weymouth, a slight blond gentleman of unquestioned good fashion and good sense, gestured to a servant to bring out another platter of beef and ham, made room for his grace and the Hon. Lionel Fitzmartin at his table. The friends spent some time in deep discussion of the finer points of horseflesh, of notorious races recently won and lost, and of the vast fortunes that had accordingly changed hands. There was a discussion of monetary matters, and then a discussion of recent weather as it could be related to agriculture and rising prices.

By then, it was time to introduce an entirely new topic—a task that Mr. Fitzmartin blithely undertook, with the assistance of a glass of ruby port.

"Well then, Sarratt, tell us," asked he, "what is the news about the succession? We're all ears to know."

"Succession, Lionel? Which succession?"

"Yours, one supposes, Charles," interjected Weymouth. "Did you not know that you and the future of the whole Wellesford lineage have become the subject of intense debate in town? In short, everyone has turned their attention toward your marital prospects."

The duke of Sarratt, displeased, paled slightly. "Indeed so?"

"The odds of your announcing your betrothal within the month are running very high! In fact, I could find no one to bet against it. I tried, I assure you."

His grace, inwardly horrified to be the object of *on dits,* and even more so to have his personal business bandied about town, smiled weakly and made no reply.

"I, of course, have tried to deny all such rumors of marriage," said Lionel, "and held that you are quite resigned to having your old and noble title pass to that unpresentable cousin of yours."

"However, no one, save myself, believes Fitzmartin's tale," added the earl of Weymouth. "I know you'll never marry, and so I've told all who ask me. Any rumor of your marriage, say I, must be sheerest nonsense, as you have been known for all your life to be the most recklessly confirmed bachelor of any in town—and have always been renowned as an outspoken, and complete misogynist."

"Quite," said the duke.

"But now, Charles, you shall tell us yourself," said Lionel. "Can this wild story that has swept through London society possibly be true? Are the hopes of some lucky mother of a young lady of quality to be realized beyond her wildest dreams? Are you soon to leave our gay society of hardened bachelors? *Are* you truly to be wed at last?"

"It *is* true that my esteemed mother would have me wed," the duke admitted, and not without difficulty.

"Your *mother?* Oh, dear—there's an end to it then. Can't go against one's own mother's wishes. If her grace is set upon your marrying, there's an end to your jolly bachelorhood. I say, bad luck, Charles. My condolences."

"I accept them," said the duke. "Indeed, I know not what other course to take than acquiescence. You cannot conceive of the pressure that dear lady has brought to bear upon me. I must, from filial duty, concede defeat at last."

"Oh, Sarratt, no!"

"Oh, Weymouth, yes! It's merely a matter of time, and so you may tell all of them who are wishing to wager their blunt, that they may as well wager it on just how soon they are to wish me joy, for I have not quite settled on the timing of that matter. Some time this year, it seems."

"Who's the lucky lady?" asked Fitzmartin.

The duke rolled his eyebrows to the ceiling and pursed his lips, saying, with forced casualness, "Oh, heaven, *I* don't know, and it's hardly the point. I've not decided. Adelaide Henchart, most likely, I suppose."

"Ooh! You're a cheeky fellow, to take her on! To marry the Henchart spitfire!" said Fitzmartin.

"Spitfire? Is she?"

"Is Lady Adelaide Henchart a spitfire? Good god, man! Is China on the other side of earth? What's the matter, man? Is the female sex *entirely* invisible to you, Charles? Of course, she's a spitfire—everyone in town knows it, man, why don't you?" said Lord Weymouth. "How can you think to marry a maiden of whom you know so little?"

"Because, James, I feel strongly that, in such matters, ignorance is bliss."

"You're quite mad, Charles. I've always said you were mad. Didn't I always say so, Lionel?"

"Always," confirmed Fitzmartin, pouring out another glass of wine.

"You should have applied yourself this season at Almack's. Told you that you should. Lots of pretty chits out this season. Why settle for Adelaide?" asked Weymouth.

"It saves me the trouble of undergoing the indignity of an entire season of balls, and breakfasts and assemblies. I'm too old for all that, and besides, I ran that gantlet in my youth. This marriage will not be built upon sentiment, but upon reason. After all, Adelaide's family is an old and distinguished one."

"Good blood there in the Hencharts. Best there is, my Aunt Mary told me," agreed Lionel. "Good blood. Old blood. Family goes back before the Conqueror. No problems there."

"Old blood? Oh, well, *that'll* make a difference in the cold, wee hours of the night!" said the earl sarcastically.

"Nothing to sneer at, Weymouth. Girl *has* to have good bloodlines. Otherwise, what's the point?" asked Lionel.

"Bloodlines?" repeated Lord Weymouth, aghast.

"Yes, bloodlines. Why not? What else is there more important to consider?"

"Beauty?" asked the earl.

"There is that," his grace conceded.

"Sensibility, perhaps?" offered Lionel.

"Rubbish. I've no sensibility at all, myself, and I won't be saddled with a wife who has!" said the duke. "Adelaide doesn't have any, does she?"

"No, she doesn't," conceded Weymouth. "Not a bit of it."

"There you are, then," said the duke, as if this explained everything. "Mind you, I haven't yet come right out and asked her, so it's not formally settled yet. It is always possible that I may throw caution to the winds and find someone else. I might even leave the decision to a passing whim, or even—to a throw of the dice.''

"Capital idea, Sarratt!" exclaimed Mr. Fitzmartin, always eager for a game of chance. "What say we make up a pool of eligible young ladies, place bets on the outcome, and in the end, you agree to marry the girl whose name we pull out of a hat! That's sporting!''

"Sporting? No, it's not at all sporting to pull names out of a hat. I think it's rather romantic," said Lord Weymouth. "In an odd way.''

"Romance doesn't suit me, James. This will be purely a business arrangement. In the case that I do take Adelaide, rest assured that she will behave like a spitfire no longer. Lady Adelaide shall promise to behave just as her husband says, or live to regret it. I'll tolerate no nonsense in my lawfully wedded wife.''

"What if she won't have you?"

The duke eyed his friend narrowly. "Don't be absurd. Of course she'll have me. Lady Adelaide Henchart, like all girls on the lookout for the best marriage they can wangle, has recurring and insatiable visions of strawberry leaves on coronets. Not wish to be the duchess of Sarratt? Absurd! She's just like all those other grasping wenches. She'd sell her immortal soul for a share of my title. Not to mention my wealth.''

"Which we won't mention," said Lionel.

The Earl of Weymouth threw up his hands at his friend's display of cynicism. "You're too much for me, Charles! You and your wretched, cynical view of women—I don't know how to account for it!" He lowered his voice and whispered to young Mr. Fitzmartin in a mock-confidential tone, "You must be aware that Sarratt's a frightful man with the women—famed for being overbearing and unmanageable! The duke of Sarratt is as ham-handed and stroppy with the fairer sex as he is light-handed with a spirited team of blood bays!''

''It's perfectly true,'' replied his grace evenly. ''I don't deny it. I have no way with women, nor have I ever wished to. I don't like the sex at all, and never have. I've no use for them. If I weren't a duke, I wouldn't consider marrying at all, for I couldn't be bothered with all their daily fusses and fits of hysterics. If it weren't for my mother still being alive, and wishing to see a grandson born before she dies, I'd not even mind about the succession. In fact, I'd rather enjoy seeing Herbert Grimwold swanning around town, borrowing to the hilt on his ducal expectations.''

The duke ceased speaking as fresh platters arrived and were placed on the table. He began to eat, finding, in his discontent, his appetite aroused.

He pointed out to his friends, ''After all, what does it signify to me if the dukedom passes to my second cousin? After I'm dead, what should I care? But Mother will have it that she sees me have a son and direct heir, and I must respect her wishes.

''Whatever my filial duty may be, however, I desire to keep my personal freedom, and I swear that when I do marry, it will be to a woman who will give me no cause for concern. She must shepherd my ward, Diana, through her first year in society, and otherwise may keep quietly in the background, like a Sevres figurine.''

''That doesn't sound a bit like our Lady Adelaide, Charles!''

''Don't be too sure. I am not devoid of weaponry. I have good reason to believe that Adelaide desires to be a duchess so very badly that she'd even sell her temper to the devil. Her social ambition is such that, in order to be referred to as 'her grace' for the remainder of her life, she would be willing to behave just exactly as would please me—and that's a good start, isn't it? I would be even more pleased by any woman ready to adhere to my motto of proper domesticity: wives should be seen and not heard. And not seen often."

A dangerous gleam danced within the duke's dark eyes. "In fact, following our esteemed Prinny's example, my principle is that one's wife should be seen in private no more often than is needful to—ah—secure an heir."

"Wicked, Sarratt, wicked!" said Fitzmartin, laughing uproariously.

"And perhaps a spare," continued his grace with a wry curl of his lips. "*One* spare."

The room filled with laughter that took some time to die down, and more food and liquor was called for to complement the high spirits of the company.

"You are an impenitent rascal, Sarratt!"

"So I am," replied his grace evenly.

"Now, tell us, did you express yourself to your esteemed mother in just those vivid terms, Charles?"

"Certainly not. It would have been most indelicate, and I am never that."

"No more you are. But I'd hate to be in your new wife's shoes—cold comfort to be your duchess, my dear Charles."

"Well, that's just how I feel about the whole sorry business. It can't be helped that I'm not in the petticoat line—it is a disinterest which happens to be an integral part of my character."

"More's the pity for you, Sarratt."

"Not at all," replied his grace. "I believe myself to be playing from a position of great strength. I have no romantic hopes or desires whatsoever, and thus am ever unable to have my hopes disappointed."

At this, the Earl of Weymouth and the Hon. Lionel

Fitzmartin both looked very thoughtful, and to their friend made no further reply. They looked at their tall companion with expressions that closely resembled compassion.

In this silence, a loud, commanding voice was heard hailing Lord Weymouth and the duke from across the room. Soon after the voice arrived, its bearer did, a beefy young gentleman with a complexion reddened by the habitual consumption of an excess of spirits.

"Henchart!" called Fitzmartin. "I heard you lost greatly betting on that bay mare that ran at Heathdown. Told you she couldn't do it, didn't I? Henchart never listens to me, either, but I was right, now wasn't I? How much blunt did you lose?"

The Hon. Roger Henchart scowled, mentioned an outrageous sum, and took a seat at the table. The duke, for his part, took the opportunity to study the countenance of the man he might all too soon have to acknowledge as a brother-in-law.

Roger Henchart was not his favorite gentleman, not by a long chalk. A gambler, a rakehell, in fact, the very model of an intemperate younger son, Henchart's main occupation in life was wagering away his family's fortune as fast and furiously as possible. In this, his chosen career, Henchart had made great progress in recent months. Roger's benighted father was well on his way to the grave from worry about the inroads being made on the family wealth. For now, it was a matter of paying off Roger's debts just as fast as he amassed them, if only to keep the family's name from scandal. Lady Rutherfurd had pinned the family's hopes on Adelaide's being able to snare the duke to wed, and had persuaded her husband, Lord Rutherfurd, that in order to further this alliance, keeping the family name unbesmirched was of absolutely paramount importance, and well worth the blunt. She knew, and rightly enough, that the duke, for all his eccentric and cold behavior toward females, would certainly not marry into scandal.

If Sarratt had liked Henchart better, he might have taken the time to point out to him the error of his ways, and steer him toward virtue and a sense of responsibility, as his father had done to him in his youth. But Sarratt did not like Roger, and never had, and thus could not be bothered to act for him. As it was, merely having to endure the boorish young man approach him at his table was more evidence of the unfortunate consequences marriage into the family of the Earl of Rutherfurd would bring him. Was there to be no way out of it? His marital imprisonment was becoming more and more a foregone conclusion.

Henchart rambled on in his egotistical way, telling tales of races and wagers won, with an eye to improving his public image, and as he did so, the Duke of Sarratt allowed his mind to wander—and not onto pretty paths. He thought of the recent spate of royal marriages that had occurred in response to the death of Princess Charlotte. One after another, the royal dukes had given in and subjected themselves to marriage in order to do their duty by the monarchy: The Duke of Kent had married Mary Victoria, Dowager Princess of Saxe-Meiningen; the Duke of Clarence wed Princess Adelaide; the Duke of Cambridge married Princess Augusta of Hesse-Cassel. None of these, of course, was a love match: even the royal dukes had, in the end, sacrificed themselves on the altar of duty. Why should the duke of Sarratt not do so as well?

He had to marry; his mother was right, he had to. Sarratt sighed. It might as well be Lady Adelaide, even if her brother was a fool soon to be entirely done up.

Knowing himself a lost man, the duke entered the lists at last by inquiring politely after the health of Henchart's sister. At this rashness, the duke's two best friends tried hard to keep amused looks off their faces, without quite succeeding.

The Hon. Roger Henchart, no fool in the ways of marital settlements, was unable to hide his own delight that such a question had occurred. It was a good sign, an excellent sign—apparently it was true that the duke was on the way, if slowly and reluctantly, toward making Adelaide an offer. It would, of course, mean a great deal to his creditors if it became known that his sister was affianced to the fabulously wealthy Duke of Sarratt.

"Adelaide's fine, Sarratt—couldn't be better. Why, just the other day she asked me if I'd seen you. I'm sure she'd like you to look in on her at Almack's—shall I tell her you'll be there this week?"

There it was. An open challenge. Best to get it over with at once.

"Ah, to be sure, Henchart. Do bring Lady Adelaide my very best regards, and tell her I shall," and here the noble duke choked, thinking of the insipid company and cloying beverages that were all that was offered there. Finally, his grace said, "Yes, Henchart, I very much look forward to seeing Lady Adelaide at the next assembly."

The Hon. Lionel Fitzmartin surreptitiously poked the earl of Weymouth in the ribs, and was rewarded for this act by a black look from the duke of Sarratt, whose knees had turned to water, and whose bile was rising in his gullet.

"Almack's, then? Shall we all be there?" asked Lionel, innocently, trying to cover his gaffe.

"Why would *you* go there, Lionel? You're not trying to find a spouse, or are you?" asked Lord Weymouth.

"I go there because I like to dance. Why should I not? What about it, Weymouth? Are you going?"

"I? I? No, I'm as bad an old bachelor as Sarratt is. Maybe worse. I have four years on him."

"Come on, Weymouth. Let's make it an evening for all of us. Come along, won't you?" asked the duke. "I need the kind support of friends."

"No, no. On that night I hope to be safely tucked away in my library planning which room I shall next have redesigned and reornamented."

"I'm sure there are a whole fleet of girls who wear the willow for you, Weymouth. Give them a second chance."

"Nonsense. They all have eyes only for you, Sarratt. You outrank me so far that, like a star next to the sun, I am outshone, and undone."

Roger Henchart looked at the duke, to see how he would take this, but the duke showed no reaction whatsoever. All things considered, it was a good sign—Henchart wanted very much for his Adelaide to snare the wealthy duke, just as did his father and his mother, and his pretty witch of a sister.

It would mean a new and even more wonderful life. His gambling career could soon take off to untold heights, with no limit on the bets he could place, and have his new brother-in-law cover. What was a pretty penny for the Earl of Rutherfurd was hardly a drop in the bucket to the grand Duke of Sarratt. It wasn't fair, this current distribution of wealth, and Roger Henchart believed in wealth's redistribution—toward him, of course. If Roger could do anything, anything at all to hasten Adelaide's marriage, he would do it. At any cost.

Chapter 3

The noises of the street seemed maddeningly loud, making even more unbearable the headache that had plagued Lady Mary Hamilton all the long journey to London. Having been unceremoniously handed down from a dilapidated hackney by a jarvey who made no secret that he had far better things to do with himself, she stood with her companion in the drizzling rain outside a great townhouse on Park Lane. The two females, seemingly a bit shocked by the newness of all that surrounded them, clutched at their reticules and hugged their cloaks against themselves in order to keep their less-than-fashionable pelisses covered against the mud and damp.

"We're so terribly late; I'm not sure how we can explain our night arrival—it's just not done, of course. The house-keeper will be sure to read you the riot act; I don't even know if I can keep Buckley from giving you a good, sound scold. Are you sure you want to go through with this, your ladyship?"

"Most certainly I do, Fanny. What should I have to

fear from a steward? After all, our tardiness was hardly our fault. If the roads hadn't been in such bad condition the coach would not have broken an axle, and we would have arrived in plenty of time, just as we planned."

"I'm afraid excuses are not what is wanted here, or expected—for only the quality can get away with keeping eccentric hours. I'll just go in ahead and see if I can put things right with Mr. Buckley."

"Please, by all means, do so, but pray hurry, Fanny," said the taller of the two as she began to head for the front entranceway, marked by a lamp and gleaming brass knocker. "I'll wait here. My head is hurting me so—if I can't lie down with a vinaigrette, I think I shall die!"

A sturdy woman of perhaps fifty years whispered to her younger companion, tugging at her drab cloak, "Not that way, your ladyship! You mustn't wait there—recall that we must use the servants' entrance."

"Well, of course we must use the servants' entrance. Do you take me for a complete flat?"

"I do not," the other replied, amused. "It is merely that your ladyship may not be acquainted with the most likely *location* of the servants' entrance, your ladyship having, to put it bluntly, only descended to your present menial position in the last few moments. Furthermore, give me leave to inform your ladyship that you are waiting patiently far too close to the formal entranceway. It is not meant for the likes of you, a mere housemaid!"

The Lady Mary Hamilton blushed, stepped back, and pulled her cloak closer about her, trying to take protection from the rain. Her soft black curls were stuck in tendrils round her face; her creamy complexion was awash with raindrops.

"Of course. You're right, as always, Fanny. The door we want to use is over this way, is it?"

"Yes, milady. In the area."

"Do stop 'miladying' me!"

"Yes, milady."

"Fanny!"

"Oh, very well."

"Go ahead in, then, Fanny. I'll be fine here; I assure you."

Mrs. Fanny Simpson left her, not without misgivings. Even though the young woman's shabby dress and damp situation were outmoded and unbecoming, it would be evident to anyone who glanced her way that the girl huddled in the cloak was very young, very lovely, and very clearly unused to the ways of the great city of London. Easy prey, in fact, so it was doubly important to get the excuses done with, and get her ladyship settled into her new situation.

It was not merely to get Lady Mary out of the London night, but to get the girl a good night's sleep, and rid her of that headache! Fanny knew what Lady Mary Hamilton did not—that the poor child would be rudely awakened at first light. Lady Mary would be off to lay the morning fires and begin the tedious round of sweeping and waxing and rubbing and polishing, counting out linens, counting out silver and dishes, laying them all out, clearing them, cleaning them, and counting them again before putting them away.

Involuntarily, Mrs. Fanny Simpson shuddered, as the memory of her own start in service, so many years ago, rose again to haunt her.

Soon, Lady Mary would be no more her own employer, but the great duke's employee, at work in a house where Fanny Simpson could protect her charge no longer. Lady Mary would soon learn about backstairs manners, morals, politics and intrigues, and all the rest of the household drama that occurred in the servants' halls—a rich history forever unknown to the quality upstairs.

At just the moment that Mrs. Fanny Simpson disap
peared within the townhouse, a carriage bearing a splendi
crest raced around the corner, drawn by a team of higl
spirited bays, splattering mud near the lovely young lad
waiting outside, who, being from up-country and unuse
to city ways, had lingered too long near the dangerou
curb.

"Heads up, there, dearie!" called the driver. "Loo
alive! London streets are for our London vehicles—you'r
like to get yourself killed standing around in the stree
at this time of night, in this weather, when no one ca
see proper to drive anyhow!"

The lady stepped back into the shadows and out c
harm's way, as a very tall figure appeared out of th
coachman's conveyance. The person who emerged fror
the modish carriage was a dark-haired, powerfully bui
gentleman, dressed to the pink, and clearly rather th
worse for wine.

Fascinated by this London creature, a fashionable mal
such as she had never before beheld, the young gi
stepped forward into a pool of light cast by th
entranceway sconces to get a better look.

A liveried footman came out of the duke's residenc
wielding an umbrella, and held it over his grace as th
Duke of Sarratt proceeded, with only a mild unsteadines
toward the front entrance of Sarratt House.

A strong feeling, an odd feeling he could not at a
account for suddenly overpowered the duke of Sarrat
and caused him to turn his head toward the street. Ther
standing in a mist of fog punctuated by rays of light, hi
grace was treated to the sight of an exquisite female, on
such as he had never before beheld.

Her skin was a pure, pale white, and framed by
waterfall of darling ebony curls. Two deep violet eye
most heavily lashed, peered out at him with frank inquis

tiveness; a playful smile danced upon two curved, blush-pink lips. She raised her eyebrows in a teasing manner, and laughed in a voice so sweet it seemed a like a magical sound bred of clear Scots brooks.

The duke's heart began to race; his breath stopped in his throat; his hands actually began to tremble. He looked at the girl with an instinctive recognition, and yet his intellect knew perfectly well that he had never seen this face before.

His grace of Sarratt, both abashed and amazed, felt a surge of deep physical desire arise within him, one such as he had not felt in all his thirty-four years of life. He stared in passionate awe at this vision of beauty and innocence, a man stupefied by what he felt and beheld.

Then, the Duke of Sarratt, knowing himself to be acting entirely out of character, yet quite unable to prevent himself, cried out, "My god, woman! Who *are* you?"

At this, Lady Mary Hamilton, taken aback, gasped, covered her mouth with her hand, and withdrew again into the shadows, trying to make herself invisible.

"Come here, I say! At once!"

Lady Mary Hamilton pressed her back against the brick wall to stay in the darkness, then slipped away and hid some few entranceways away, where she could still see the duke, but where she was too far away from him to hear his words precisely. She realized that the shock of running into her new employer without warning had driven her headache completely out of her mind. Her mind held thoughts only of the duke, but she knew she must hide from him.

The Duke of Sarratt, on his part, was trying to bring the unusual vision he had beheld back into focus. He blinked his eyes; when he was able to focus them once again, his vision of beauty was still utterly vanished. He staggered a step or two in the girl's direction, toward the darkness. He rubbed his eyes, and peered off into the eerie night again.

"I say! Girl! Are you there still? Girl! Speak to me! Answer! By God, you must and shall answer me!"

But the devastated Duke of Sarratt was speaking only to the fog.

As he realized this, he grew agitated, and started pacing back and forth in front of the door, worrying his porter not a little. His grace's head began to pound almost unendurably, and his thoughts plummeted into a wild confusion.

"Gone, has she? Gone away? Or is it rather that the girl was a mere apparition, indeed a spirit, which simply vanished into the emptiness from which it came? Truly, I must be more foxed than I knew. What a fool am I to stand here in front of my ancestral home, trying to entice a comely wraith into conversation.

"What can have come over me? Love at first sight? What a splendid fit of madness this is!

"Most diverting, really. If I were not sure that I have just now experienced a powerful hallucination of my brain, which occurred due to recent consumption of an excess of port wine, I should think my poor heart might have been entrapped, well and truly."

The duke laughed ruefully at himself, and at his odd experience.

"Ah, well, here's a swift end to a mad dream. Reality shall now assume its proper dominance, thank god, and I'll be safe once more from all women and their wiles."

The Duke of Sarratt recovered his composure and dashed inside his house, his mind indulging itself in hurried contemplation of ideas that arose as a direct result of his recent ingestion of French wine. Then a thought occurred to him with great force: it might be high time that he reduce sharply his consumption of spirituous liquors.

* * *

Fanny Simpson emerged from the servants' entrance just in time to witness the duke's none-too-steady retreat into his town mansion. So that was the distinguished Duke of Sarratt, the head of the household Lady Mary was to enter in service? That was the duke, leering at poor, unprotected Lady Mary, on first sight of her? To top it off, the fellow had clearly been in his cups, as well.

It was all too disturbing; what would happen next?

When Fanny's mind turned to those dreadful Aylestons, she became even more anxious. Those two wretched, mercenary beasts had nearly succeeded in their scheme to control the Hamilton fortunes—why, that whole plot to carry her off had been outrageous! They belonged in Newgate.

The worst danger to Lady Mary Hamilton, Fanny knew, was the effect her beauty had upon the male sex. As example, she had only to think back a few moments to the gleam of desire she had seen in the eyes the Duke of Sarratt the first moment he saw her.

It was the fault of the Marton looks, of course: they had caused the Marton women problems over many generations. In her youth, Lady Mary's mother was Lady Elizabeth Marton, famed across the country for her exotic, fabulous, breathtaking beauty. Lady Mary Hamilton, with her violet eyes and ebony hair, was the very image of her dear departed mother. It had been one thing when such astonishing beauty was hidden away at Danby Court in Cumberland; but now that she had come to London, every man within a half mile was a threat.

Fanny's thoughts were interrupted by her ladyship, who had re-emerged from hiding into the light. A distinctly mischievous smile was playing upon her ruby-red lips. Seeing the girl, Mrs. Fanny Simpson's mind was quickly lifted out of low spirits, helped by the infectious, natural joy that pervaded Mary's very being. That, in combination with her beauty, would make men fall in love with her in an instant, and would make most young women hate her on first sight.

"Fanny! Did you see him?" demanded Lady Mary. "Did you not see him just now, Fanny?"

"See whom?" said Fanny, though she knew the answer perfectly well.

"My new employer, silly! The Duke of Sarratt!" The girl clapped her hands with delight, and gave out a high trill of laughter.

"I did," replied Fanny Simpson with a wary look.

"Just a trifle *bosky,* wasn't his grace?" remarked Lady Mary saucily. "Would strip to advantage however, I should think!"

" 'Strip to advantage!' 'Bosky!' Lady Mary! Where *did* you learn such language?" cried out her faithful governess.

"Not from you, certainly. Don't you like my new figures of speech? I'm trying out my downstairs vocabulary. I think I may possess a distinct talent for it. What is your opinion?"

"Don't you dare pick up any such vulgarisms. I won't have it—that's my opinion! Do you hear, your ladyship? 'Bosky!' Of all words!"

"Well, but he *was!* Or does he say such things to all the girls?"

"Don't be pert! And don't think you're too old for me to box your ears!"

"You're such a tyrant, Fanny," said Lady Mary fondly. "You may box my ears, if it pleases you."

"Enough! You are being foolish beyond permission. What I need to know is just what things did that man say to you? Was he very forward?"

"Not at all."

"You're fibbing—I can see it in your eyes. Oh, I *knew* this plan was doomed, and I said so from the start."

"I'm not fibbing, Fanny! I would tell you if I were; I always have. No, his grace didn't *say* anything, precisely, but he did shout at me, demanding to know who I was. He was most ferocious, and I was most surprised. I can't think why he did it—perhaps a surfeit of sherry? It was quite a diverting scene, I can tell you, and the fun of it has entirely healed my headache, I am glad to say."

"I can't like it. I had much rather your headache was healed by hartshorn than by a man's lascivious glances."

" 'Lascivious glances'? My, my, Fanny—*now* who's bringing up topics quite unsuited to my young and innocent ears?"

"That will do, young lady!" huffed the steadfast governess.

Lady Mary merely smiled again, and gestured toward the rear of the house, where a small door indicated the entrance to the servants' hall.

With marked reluctance, Fanny handed over to Lady Mary a small, shabby brown portmanteau.

"It should really be a tin trunk, you know, my dear."

"Well, I don't have one, so this will have to do."

The transfer completed, any remaining trace of good humor faded from Fanny Simpson's countenance.

"There's still time to back out of this scheme, Lady Mary. I'm worried, and I won't try to hide it. I was afraid we shouldn't have come down to London, and now that we're here, I'm sure of it. I think we should have hid you in the country. It's still not too late. Are you quite sure you want to go through with this?"

"I am. Hiding in the country just wouldn't answer, Fanny. In the country, Sir Barton would track us down straightaway; be assured of it. He has men everywhere in his pay. In London I can remain anonymous. In the backstairs of a great London townhouse, I shall be entirely invisible! There will be no one here to carry tales of Lady Mary Hamilton back to Sir Barton and to Gervase at Danby Court.''

''There must be some old friends of your mother's in London. You could contact them, and arrange to stay with a good family, could you not? You might live there quietly and avoid society, mightn't you?''

''Arrive without notice on someone's doorstep? Without proper introduction, claiming acquaintance through a dead woman they haven't even heard of for ten or twenty years? No, I could not. Even if I could, I would have to explain the sordid details of my predicament. That would be the end of me forever, and of any chance of future happiness. Once the precise story of my flight from my stepfather became commonly known, it would have such scandal value that it would spread all over town in a minute—and that *would* ruin me in the eyes of society *forever.*''

''I suppose so.''

''That is the way it is with society—no matter that I was blameless in all respects, my name would be the one besmirched.''

''True.''

''No, Fanny, you must see that this present plan is much the better one.''

''But how will you survive?''

''I'll do perfectly well. I'm not an entirely useless, frivolous creature.''

''No, but you've been reared in a most genteel fashion, just as became the daughter of an earl.''

''I suppose I must consider myself fortunate that my kind and considerate stepfather vouchsafed *that* at least,'' said Lady Mary bitterly.

"So he did. Think on it well, my lady: if your ladyship can't endure the rigors of a stagecoach journey without getting a headache, how shall you ever survive, even for two months, working your hands to the bone as a lower servant? I'm sorry that I consented to the whole mad scheme," said Fanny Simpson glumly. "If one of the footmen doesn't try to take advantage of you, which of course someone must, all that heavy work will give you a chill. Then you'll take sick and die of the fever."

"Don't say such things! We've been through this again and again, Fanny, every mile of the way down here. I must stay in a place where I am quite unknown, and where Sir Barton and Gervase will not hear word of me. The idea of hiding in the guise of a housemaid is perfectly brilliant. It's like hiding a treasure in broad daylight, in plain view. I can live here quietly and simply, and do my work, and no one will know the better—certainly not those two brigands. And after all, it's only for a short time. Once I turn twenty-one, I can go to my solicitors and claim my fortune."

"It sounds a pretty plan. But what if something goes wrong?"

"What can go wrong but Sir Barton finding me, and abducting me yet again to have me wed his dreadful nephew?"

"I can think of so many it unnerves me, but those two are the heart and soul of the trouble, aren't they? Very well, your ladyship. If your mind is set on this, we'd best get you settled in. I've spoken with the steward, Mr. Buckley—he says he'll overlook your tardiness today, but should it happen again, you're in for more than just a scolding."

Lady Mary Hamilton looked nonplused for a moment. She then objected, saying, "Scolding? Oh, no, that won't do at all! I shan't like that! I don't at all care for being scolded, Fanny."

"No more does anyone, Lady Pea-goose. When you're scolded, you mind your tongue! You'd best not act as if you were quality—you'll give yourself away in an instant. You know your place, and be humble. If you can't, this whole charade is useless."

"Too true. Only think what would happen if I were to be caught! The news of Lady Mary Hamilton being caught play-acting the part of a maid would spread like wildfire throughout London. That would make a scandal, too—it's horrible to contemplate."

"You must behave like a real servant. Learn to be meek, deferential, conformable, and not to be encroaching."

"Encroaching? I? Why, I'd die first!" said Lady Mary with an outraged glance at her companion. "What a thing to say, Fanny! You'd think I'd been brought up in a stable! I'm *never* encroaching!"

"No more you are. But you aren't at all used to having to efface yourself, and when your temper is overset—you're quite a handful, my Lady Mary Hamilton, if I may be so bold as to say so."

"Abuse me to my face? Oh, all right, go ahead, tease me about my temper. You always are bold enough to say whatever you wish, Fanny. You've been riding roughshod over me ever since I was in leading-strings."

Fanny grinned, but did not reply directly to this criticism, offering additional advice instead.

"As a proper domestic in one of London's greatest households, you must efface yourself. Only think of the Duke of Exfort! If he so much as catches a glimpse of a housemaid in the family's rooms, the maid is dismissed on the spot! You will have to see if Sarratt is as fussy as Exfort, but certainly you must know your place. You must be invisible: it is the key to successfully fulfilling your position in the house. *And* to ensuring your own personal safety."

"My safety?"

"Of course. If you can pass yourself off as a real servant, you will be safe from the Aylestons. If you can become an exemplary servant, one who performs her tasks invisibly, one whose character is known to be above reproach, you will be safe from all the manservants in the household."

"Nonsense. What are you suggesting? Who would dare to bother me?"

"Who would dare? Don't be naive. Look at what just happened to you—your own employer ogled you within seconds of your arrival at his house."

"Fanny! I wouldn't say that his grace 'ogled' me, precisely. I would say that he merely cast me a—how shall I put it? That his grace cast me a . . . highly *appreciative* glance."

"Will you *please* pay attention, Lady Mary? The consequences to your virtue and reputation could be serious. You must attend, milady, and appreciate the circumstances for what they are."

Lady Mary waited with a touch of impatience for the inevitable advice to come.

"You are now at Sarratt House, Lady Mary, one of the very greatest of the London townhouses, requiring a small army of servants to run it. The majority of this army is male. There are footmen, running footmen, stewards, coachmen, stable-boys, lamp-lighters, valets, and under-butlers. Every one of them might possibly—how shall I put it?—be the cause of certain *difficulties*. Not to mention the quality."

"Nonsense, Fanny! None of them would dare to try to take liberties with me! Surely not!"

"Don't be a ninnyhammer! Once you enter within,

Lady Mary, you no longer qualify as quality; any man who is inclined to dare to take liberties with a girl is well within his rights to do so. Once inside that house, a girl must learn to protect her own virtue, for no one else will care a fig about it. No one cares, except that if one is thought to be fast, one will be fast dismissed. As a maid, a pretty maid at that, you must learn straightaway how to fend men off, and not just in the subtle ways that generally suffice for gentlemen of good breeding."

"Then I shall learn to take care of myself. I held my own with Gervase, after all, did I not?"

"You did, indeed. Gervase by then had certainly doffed *any* pretense of gentlemanly behavior."

"Ill-bred brute! Those twenty-four hours in which I was trapped in his company, racing toward Gretna Green, were the most horrible of my life. That time was quite enough to unveil to me the darker side of the male sex. You need not worry, Fanny, for at Sarratt House, I shall be ever wary and always act wisely, I promise you. I shall act to protect my good name and my virtue, even though no one else knows or cares about it."

"Very good, my lady."

"Thank you, Fanny." The young girl held her hand out to open the door, and then hesitated. She drew back toward her longtime governess and friend.

"My heart's racing, Fanny. I find I'm frightened—and I'm so reluctant to leave you, my dear friend. Oh, do wish me luck!"

"Best wishes. Don't be afraid."

"I'm afraid I shall give myself away in the first ten minutes. Do you think I shall?"

"Certainly not. Say as little as possible; maintain a low profile, and do as you're told. Cultivate a meek countenance."

"*That* shall prove a challenge," said Lady Mary with

a wry look, but Fanny ignored her charge and continued on.

"Beware of becoming the object of household gossip, and beware your fellow staff. Be slow to cultivate friendships till you know the character of those you wish to befriend. As to the rest of your problems with your inheritance, we must hope and pray that this situation will provide the protection that you require until you reach your majority."

"It will work, Fanny; I feel very confident about it. Sir Barton will never think to search for me in such reduced circumstances."

"So long as you remain at Sarratt House, you will be safe from Sir Barton. However, you must succeed at your work to succeed in your deception. Try to make the best of it. Master the arts and sciences of polishing and sweeping."

"I will, Fanny. It is only a matter of two months. I feel sure that I can learn to mix beeswax and turpentine, and shine up a brass knocker to lucent perfection."

"Indeed, Lady Mary? And what about carrying down bath slops, and emptying spittoons?"

"Spittoons?" cried the Lady Mary Hamilton, as a look of deep revulsion spread across her lovely features.

"What, child, did you think spittoons emptied of their own volition?"

"I confess I had not previously given the matter much thought."

Mrs. Fanny Simpson suppressed a hearty laugh, saying, "I should suppose not. At any rate, we must thank heaven that you've not been engaged to work in the scullery; there, things could be much worse. We must hope that Buckley and Mrs. Brindle will take quick notice of your gentle manners, and not set you to servicing the honey-buckets."

Lady Mary Hamilton grimaced again and then shuddered deeply, adding, "As to the work and the company, I don't fear them—I used to help out in the stables at Danby Court. In fact, old Burton insisted that I do so, as a matter of horsemanship. But it's true enough that I know nothing at all about how to perform the tasks for which I have been engaged."

"You'll learn soon enough—or they will sack you."

"Sack me?" the young lady asked, incredulous. "What do you mean, 'sack me'? Dismiss me? Oh, surely not!"

"They will if they think you a slacker."

"I'm *not* a slacker! What a thing to say!"

"That is the way of things for servants. In fact, it may be enlightening for your ladyship to see how the other half lives."

"See it? I must, perforce, live it. I shall learn. I shall be fine."

"All right, then. We have stayed here nattering much too long as it is. I must wake up the hackney jarvey and go to my family, and you must go within. I'll write when I can."

She kissed her charge on the cheek, whispering, "Good luck, Lady Mary."

"Please, Fanny!" the girl whispered back. "Don't say that! I am 'Lady Mary' no longer!"

And in an instant, it was so.

Chapter 4

The Lady Mary Hamilton, impulsive scion of the noble house of Hamilton, brave heiress fled to London from the north, received her first really dreadful scolding immediately upon entering the back hall. It was delivered with loud and thundering authority by Mr. Buckley, the duke's chief steward, ably assisted in this task by the terrifying Mrs. Rose Brindle, red-haired head housekeeper of Sarratt House. The subject of their dual admonition was that punctuality was expected of all of the servants of Sarratt House, regardless of weather, other unforeseeable conditions, or anything else at all, in fact.

The two heads of the great household also let Lady Mary (now called simply "Mary Simpson") know that it was both dangerous and improper for females to wander around late at night in London, however one might have been used to behaving in the country. Buckley and Mrs. Brindle told Mary that any such actions in the future would not be tolerated, and would lead to instant dismissal.

Poor gentle Lady Mary was devastated by being the

object of such a dressing down; so much so, that she spoke not a word in her own defense. It was as well she hadn't spoken, for even if she had, no one would have listened to her. Why should they? The girl was just another drudge, and Sarratt House was full of them, like other noble households of London, and like all the other great households all across England.

In fact, Sarratt House was, unlike most London homes, much more on the scale of a large country house; the land on Park Lane had been granted to the Wellesford family a long time ago, and even compared to other great town mansions, it was vast. There had been sufficient money in the ducal family to raise a great mansion on that land, and then to maintain it in the very first style of fashion over many years, employing an extensive staff.

Keeping the quality (and their possessions) in the manner to which they were accustomed was a task of no small proportion. In an age when one might be called upon to entertain as many as fifteen hundred persons of an evening, there had to be sufficient staff on hand, sufficiently trained to handle such events. Sarratt House, however pinchpenny other so-called noble houses might be, never stooped to borrowing footmen or other staff. Such economies were unnecessary, given the vastness of the fortune which had been left the current duke by his provident forebears.

The house had always to be maintained in proper order, which took some doing, as it was filled, if not with antiquities, certainly with *objets d'art* which required meticulous care. The architecture was rather masterful—keeping all those gilt-covered chairs and ceiling carvings clean required an army of careful and dedicated workers.

It was this army into which the Lady Mary Hamilton had been conscripted. Her ladyship's career as a servant almost having ended on the day it began, Sarratt House's newest maid ascended to her dark, drab bedroom at the very top of the house, dragging her baggage behind her as she went.

Wearily she put herself to bed, doing this for the very first time in her entire life. What had begun as rather an entertaining adventure was turning out to be most unentertaining reality.

In her tiny, shabby room at the top of the house, she found her crude bed. Safely inside the cold coarse sheets, shivering and miserable, Lady Mary discovered another unpleasant fact of her new life: her bed held another occupant, one Susan Bowker, the second housemaid, who not only outranked her by two levels, but who was very highly irritated at having to let Mary into her bed.

"You the new one?" she grumbled. "You must be. Get on in, then, don't be slow about it. Hey, you're letting all the warm air out. Take care not to hog all the blankets, d'ye hear me? I'll pinch you if I catch you with all the warm things on your side; I promise I'll pinch you black and blue."

The Lady Mary Hamilton was horrified at this pronouncement, but replied in her customarily civil tone, "Good-night, then, Susan."

"Aw, pipe down, jaw-me-dead," growled her unappreciative new bedfellow. "Pipe *down,* fer the love of heaven!"

Dawn broke at the accustomed instant, but was accompanied by no arrival of a steaming porcelain ewer in which gentle Lady Mary might make her morning ablutions. There was no maid to help dress her, and no decent dresses in which she might dress: only the dowdy hand-me-down frocks that Fanny Simpson had secured for her use.

She rose from her bed with reluctance, noting that the

space on the far side was evidence that Susan Bowker had gone down already. Lady Mary felt not at all the thing; her back ached from sleeping on the thin, lumpy flock mattress, and, though it was April, it was still dark out and damp and cold, and she was chilled to the bone. She felt her nose beginning to run, and she reached for her handkerchief.

Looking at the intricate lace that surrounded the square of fine linen, she sighed and blew delicately. What was this unwelcoming new world into which she had thrust herself? How was she ever to make her way in it?

With Susan Bowker safely gone, Lady Mary took the opportunity to feel around in her case to check on her black velvet bag. It was there, just where she had put it; the jewels were safe, thank heaven. Hoping no one would interrupt her, she turned the bag upside down and let the precious ornaments spill out onto the bed.

To strangers, they looked only like a fabulous collection of heirloom jewelry, but to Lady Mary Hamilton, they represented family, and memory, and love that lasted beyond the grave. A tear slipped down her cheek as she remembered the last time she had seen her darling mother clasp the heavy emerald necklace around her neck, adding the earrings, and the bracelet, and the ring. There was the Hamilton ruby; the double strand of pearls; the sapphire set; the emerald set; the pearl set; and the set of flawless, sparkling diamonds.

When she heard her name called roughly, she swept the jewelry back into the bag and stuffed it in the bottom of her leather case. She had no time for tears, and no time for nostalgia. She had a part to play, and much depended on her success at playing it.

Lady Mary dressed as fast as ever she could, her fingers almost unable to manage the fastenings in the cold, then smoothed her hair into a knot, and made her way down the many flights of stairs.

A young girl who was sweeping the servants' hall staircase called out to her, "Hustle up, there. You're the new Mary, aren't you? You're wanted in Mrs. Brindle's room, straightaway. It's down at the end of the hall, right there. Good luck! Just say 'Yes, ma'am' to whatever she says, and it'll go right fer ya."

"Thanks," said Lady Mary, with gratitude.

She fairly ran to the housekeeper's room, where there were two other newcomers—two beefy, young countrified-looking girls who were trying to stifle their yawns, to present a good appearance to Mrs. Brindle, who had just come in.

The housekeeper first looked the new recruits up and down, checking their hands and fingernails. She ran an eye over their clothes, pulling up an apron here, and brushing out wrinkles with her hard, firm hands. Finally, the housekeeper was ready to make her speech.

"Welcome to Sarratt House, then" she said in a brisk tone. "I am Mrs. Brindle, and you will address me as such. Our steward is Mr. Buckley, and will be known to you by that title. You will meet the rest of the staff as you proceed in your work.

"Now, I know that working in a great house is not what any of you has been used to."

"True, all too true," mumbled a weary Lady Mary under her breath.

"Silence!"

Lady Mary bit her tongue, blushed red, and Mrs. Brindle continued, with undisguised pride.

"Some of you are new to service, and some of you are not. Regardless of which is the case, you are all new to service at Sarratt House. Attend to my words: you now are part of one of the greatest households in the entire country, that of his grace the Duke of Sarratt.

"That being the case, we expect you to learn to conduct yourselves with propriety at all times. This is not a country town: it is a noble household. Singing during work, gossiping with friends, is not done here. A formal and correct demeanor is to be maintained by all staff at all times. Is that clear?"

No one answered her.

"Cleanliness is expected of all staff here, as is continually sober, modest, honest behavior. You will be taught the higher modes of behavior suitable to those who will interact with the polite world.

"As to the expected polite modes of address, these are to be observed at all times. In the event that one of you encounters the Duke of Sarratt, he is properly addressed as 'your grace' or as 'sir.' His grace's mother, the dowager duchess, is 'your grace,' or, simply 'ma'am.' The duke's ward, Miss Diana Leigh, is to be addressed as 'Miss Diana.'

"With respect to the ducal family's privacy: you must respect it. First and foremost, learn to stay out of the family's way. You may not speak unless spoken to, not ever, ever, ever. When in the presence of family or company, you may not appear in any way to have heard what has been said. No matter what is said, take no notice of it: you must not laugh at jokes, no matter how humorous; you must not respond in any way, unless it is directly asked of you by one of the family, or some one of their friends. Whatever you may come to learn in the course of carrying out your duties is not to be taken backstairs and bandied about; you are most severely forbidden to discuss the family's business—not with staff here, and certainly not with anyone else."

No one abides by that rule, I'll wager, thought Lady

Mary to herself. *I'll bet everyone knows everyone else's business, top and down and sides of it.*

Mrs. Brindle went on, "If, in the normal course of your duties, you do encounter one of the family, you are to curtsey at once. If you are in a hallway when they walk through it, curtsey quickly, and then flatten yourself against the wall so the family member may pass by unmolested. You shall leave all family rooms just as soon as your tasks have been completed, not lingering there for any reason.

"Never hand things to a family member directly—use a silver salver for newspapers and mail, or if a salver is unsuitable, merely lay the object down on a table so the family member may pick it up of his own volition.

"Noisiness will not be tolerated. You are not to call to other staff from one room to another; you are not to chatter while you work. You are to maintain and uphold the quiet dignity of Sarratt House."

Mrs. Brindle assumed a particularly theatrical tone, saying, "It is a great thing, you understand, and a great challenge to the will to perform effectively in service. Service requires that one efface oneself, doing so in service to a greater cause. In service, you must be discreet. You must be silent. You must be invisible."

"You must be . . ." and here she stopped, and looked around, as if seeking inspiration, which soon enough was found.

"Be . . . as a vase, or a lamp, or a curtain!" she cried out in triumph. "Leave your old, tawdry selves behind, and become a family ornament, an *objet d'art,* voiceless and serene."

Voiceless and serene?

It was the outside of enough. Lady Mary's eyes began to water, and, holding her breath in, she began to make a soft, choking sound. Possessed of a sharp sense of the ridiculous—a trait clearly not shared by Mrs. Brindle—she was hard put to hold in check the riotous laughter that was brimming forth within her. Perhaps out of compassion, or perhaps merely from a more innate sense of propriety, the girl next to her kicked Mary hard in the shins in an effort to silence her. Lady Mary was shocked into an awareness of where she was and who she had become, and thus she was able, with some effort, to suppress further reaction.

"In summary, girls, listen well," said Mrs. Brindle. "If children in a polite family are to be seen and not heard, the servants in the family, particularly the Lower Five, are *not* to be seen, and *not* to be heard. Is that quite clear? They are certainly not to be heard *from,* not at any time. Is that clear?"

"Yes, ma'am," sounded the three young voices, in bored unison.

"Very well then. Come here, and I shall assign each of you her duties."

The other two bobbed a curtsey to Mrs. Brindle, in which Lady Mary swiftly joined, and the working day began in earnest. They all trooped off to get the next meal's dishes, going to a massive, glass-enclosed cupboard thirty feet long by fourteen feet high, where all the fine china was kept safely locked away. Lady Mary wondered how they put anything away on the topmost shelves, they were so far from the ground. Would she have to go up a ladder? Mightn't one drop something? It was a daunting thought.

She made it through that first day, heaven knew how. She had been laboring for longer than sixteen hours, and by the time she dragged her heavy feet all the way up to her attic room again, and settled in for the night next to

Susan Bowker, she was so tired she was on the point of tears.

Lying there in her chilly room, exhausted, friendless, the sounds of the alien London streets far beneath her, she began to recall the events that had brought her to this turn. So as not to wake Susan, who would surely scold her, Lady Mary began to cry silently, tears of shame and anger and fear pouring down her cheeks. She remembered who she had become, and she remembered, all too well, the person she had once been: Lady Mary Hamilton, daughter of the Right Honorable Earl of Hamilton, and his wife, Elizabeth, of Danby Court and Hamilton House, London.

She must keep the threat of Sir Barton and Gervase constantly in mind, and keep her mind sharply set on her prime goal: avoiding his pursuit of her, avoiding falling into his trap.

Thoughts about the duke and this household—all these were extraneous to her plan for survival, one which must succeed at all costs, lest she be lost forever to herself, just as had happened to her own dear mother.

She would contrive to elude them, somehow; she had vowed on her mother's grave that she would succeed; she would not be enticed, or tricked, or forced into a miserable marriage.

Grimly conscious of that near escape, she pulled the bedcovers around her. All things considered, it was better to spend one's whole life in service rather than to be condemned to serve as the wife of Gervase Ayleston for the rest of one's existence.

When she thought of how close she had come to that, she winced. When she thought of how hard those two would pursue her trail, she wished for the oblivion of sleep, and mercifully, this was soon granted to her.

Chapter 5

Within her first fortnight, the Lady Mary Hamilton had been driven nearly out of her mind. She rose at dawn to bring up hot water in heavy five-gallon brass cans so that the quality might have warm water with which to wash. She carried the gray, cold, filthy water down again when they were done, emptied them, cleaned them, and then had to polish the cans till they shone.

Through the days, she scrubbed, and she polished, and she dusted, and she sorted, and she sewed. She ironed, and she aired, and she straightened up, and she rearranged. And when it all became dirty, or dull, or disordered, or worn, or wrinkled, or musty, or messy once more, she performed precisely the same tasks all over again.

She learned to cope with the servants' own social hierarchy: she never mixed with the "Upper Ten,"—the steward, Mr. Buckley; the housekeeper, Mrs. Brindle; the duke's valet, Boswell; and the duchess's dresser, Farley, foremost among them. Lady Mary never even ate her meals with them, but ate separately with the "Lower

Five" in the servants' hall, served by the hall porter and the hall boys. While the Upper Ten were served wine with their meals, the Lower Five made do with beer—a beverage Lady Mary found extremely distasteful.

She soon learned of all the jealousies among the servants, particularly among the housemaids: it became apparent, for example, that Susan Bowker disliked her, not because she didn't work hard, but because Mary had more gentle manners, and Susan was afraid she would win promotion ahead of her because of that. Particularly in a large household such as the duke's, promotion from within was the best way to better oneself. Over a course of years, one could reasonably hope to rise even from scullery maid to housemaid to head housemaid to ladies' maid or head housekeeper; or from the scullery to kitchen maid to cook's helper to cook to housekeeper. All these ascendancies were dependent upon acquiring gentility of manner, speech, and behavior, and upon a reputation for loyal, honest, hard work.

Hard work? Lady Mary Hamilton knew all about it. In the evening, she lit the candles, and she snuffed them at night. In the mornings, she helped collect the candlesticks and cleaned them of hardened wax, and then she polished them until they shone. She carried heavily laden breakfast trays and tea trays up several flights of backstairs, and gave them over to the higher servants who carried them in to the quality. She received from the higher servants heavily laden breakfast trays and tea trays, once the quality was done with them, and carried them down several flights of stairs back down to the kitchen again.

She helped light countless fires, she opened shutters and closed them, she drew drapes open and shut. She kneeled for hours as she scattered damp tea-leaves onto miles of carpets, and then carefully brushed them clean again. Other carpets had to be beaten rather than brushed, sometimes with beer.

Lady Mary Hamilton swept stairs and dusted stairs; she carried coals and carried logs. She polished floors on her knees with her own mixture of beeswax and turpentine, pushing a lighted candle ahead of her as she went. She, like the others working there, lived in fear that hot candlewax might drop from her candle onto a priceless carpet if she, through careless inattention, failed to hold it perfectly upright.

Her hands and knees were soon rubbed raw, as was her disposition. Tired when she had first arrived after her long flight from Danby Court to London, she was now fatigued well beyond exhaustion—her heroic efforts to complete her work quickly and properly were never enough to satisfy her peers.

Susan Bowker, in fact, had already twice discussed the fourth housemaid's sluggishness with Mrs. Brindle, and this with an eye toward instigating the demotion of the newcomer to scullery maid. According to Susan's heated analysis, blackening the grates was the only work that Mary was fit for. Lady Mary, aware of the roots of Susan's jealousy, tried to ignore her provocations.

The other servants had begun to think of Mary as rather a cold fish, but in truth, she was too tired to enter much into the servants' conversations. Sleep became the whole focus of her existence; she began to long for it, and to find in sleep her only joy.

Lady Mary Hamilton began to believe she had personally polished every single tarnished piece of silver, had swept every floor an infinite number of times, and polished with beeswax every single piece of furniture, though this was an exaggeration born of despair and fatigue. She consoled herself with the thought that the completion of every day brought her closer and closer to liberation.

And what of the handsome duke, he who had so admired Lady Mary on catching first sight of her? Every so often, the image of that unusual and arresting maiden would arise in his grace's mind, and with the image arose a feeling of longing to encounter the mysterious wraith once again. But, as he still believed her to be a creature born of fantasy, those daydreams passed quickly away.

The Duke of Sarratt was, quite naturally, unaware of Lady Mary's separate existence, though she was living only a few dozen yards away from him, toiling away there in the other world, behind the green baize door. For the first two weeks she was there, neither the duke nor any member of his family had even once laid eyes upon their new girl.

The duke was living his life as he always had—trying to make his estates more profitable, buying a horse or two, going to Jackson's, going to the club, listening patiently to his mother's continuing lectures on marriage, playing the odd game of cards now and again with Weymouth and Fitzmartin. His grace was untroubled by life, as he had always been.

It was just those dreams that kept troubling him—in dreams the woman he remembered came to him, appeared to him. She called his name, and insisted that he come to her. When he saw her in his dreams, his body was so overcome with feeling that he trembled in her presence.

But when the duke awoke, he was unable to remember what his dream had been about at all. He remembered nothing about where he had been, who he had seen, how he had felt about her.

It was only a strange, uneasy, painful feeling in his heart—one that stayed with him after he awoke, a restless feeling of full longing that remained with him all day and that could not be satisfied.

Chapter 6

There came a day toward the end of April when Lady Mary Hamilton, the new under-housemaid, finally emerged from the relative darkness of the servants' corridors out into the elegant, polished, well-lit chambers and corridors of the great ducal residence.

This rise in domestic status happened as a result of a series of unrelated and seemingly insignificant incidents. Young Jane Marshman, the red-handed, red-nosed, never-too-tidy scullery maid was late one day in getting the potatoes peeled, and, in her haste to deliver the finished, white and shining products of her hard labor back to impatient Cook, was neglectful in cleaning up the stone-flagged floor afterward.

Jane's oversight caused Ellen Hamsey, the maid who normally took service trays in to her grace, to take a nasty fall on one of those potato skins. Helen's fall onto the hard floor resulted in a slight but unsightly epistaxis.

With no other girls being well enough dressed or available to fill in for Helen, Mrs. Brindle heaved a great sigh and decided that letting an inexperienced but pretty, well-mannered, and really very surprisingly well-spoken new maid upstairs was preferable to sending up an experienced maid with an unreliable nose.

Which is, of course, how Lady Mary wound up making rather an enemy of Lady Adelaide Henchart.

Mary had, in her two weeks' time, never before been required to go beyond the servants' quarters. Being asked to take a great tray of tea and cups and beautiful little frosted seed-cakes up to her grace's sitting-room was therefore a signal honor, and a task that Mary hoped to complete with dignity and success.

But this, alas, was not to be.

It was one of those days that Lady Adelaide had designated as a visiting day. She had come ostensibly to pay a morning call on her grace, the Dowager Duchess of Sarratt, and young Miss Diana Leigh, and inform them of the news in town. In fact, Lady Adelaide had come for the reason which always impelled her to Sarratt House—in hopes of being able to run across the object of her matrimonial desires during the course of her visit.

It was the simple strategy she had selected to move her toward her ultimate goal. Lady Adelaide was too clever to throw herself at the duke in the common way of young ladies, flirting and simpering, hanging on his arm and recounting to him his virtues. Neither could she expect the noble duke to hang after her like a puppy in love, bringing her roses and compliments: he was simply not that sort of person. Lady Adelaide's deadly serious, most subtle campaign to attach the man was rather in the manner of small drops of water that would, over time, wear away at even the most adamantine boulder. Her visit brought her, once again, into his presence, and this in order to remind him once again, but gently, of her existence. In time, it would work: Lady Adelaide was sure of it.

She never tried to push Sarratt to declare himself, as might a greener girl, but neither would she let the man out of her sight for more than two days at a time. She wished to be subtle but at the same time, to be inexorable. In time, she felt, provided she was patient, the man would bow to the inevitable, and ask for her hand. She would become her grace, Adelaide, Duchess of Sarratt, with all the wonderful things that rank entailed.

With these thoughts firmly in her mind, and having dressed with particular care, one can easily image how her pride must have been soaring on that day. She, Lady Adelaide Henchart, was the closest thing to a fiancée the bachelor duke had ever had, a position worthy of respectful admiration throughout the reaches of the ton.

Lady Adelaide Henchart had dressed in a shockingly dear new green gown, which was perhaps just a little too frilly to become her, and had puffs on the shoulder ends of the sleeves that made her appear rather beefy.

Blissfully unaware of this, she ascended the great stairs of Sarratt House with dignity and confidence, displaying a broad, self-satisfied smile. These stairs, it should be noted, were famous among those addicted to the intricacies of architecture, having been designed by Ellis Arden. They had been very expensively fashioned of highly polished Italian marble.

Besides this slippery marble, the real villain of that day was Lady Vanity. Surely it was due to her baneful influence that led Lady Adelaide to hesitate in front of a splendid golden mirror to check the effect of her smile. This checking for effect led her to linger near an interesting hidden door that led to the servants' halls behind.

The staircase door, appropriately hidden in the wainscoting, had a nasty habit of sticking shut; everyone had been warned about this propensity by the under-butler. Thus, when Mrs. Brindle sent Mary up with the tea tray, following the dowager's command, the hidden door was flung open from within by a smart kick from Mary.

The wretched door then swung too far open on its hinges, and cracked Lady Adelaide smartly on her posterior as she was leaning over toward the pier-glass mirror.

When struck so rudely, her ladyship shrieked, turned around sharply, and stepped hard onto the piped hem of her own dress. Stepping again to right herself, she instead stepped on her hem again, ripping it awfully, and stood, badly balanced on the edge of the marble stairs, crying out, ''No-oo!''

Mary shifted the dangerously heavy tea tray onto one hip, so as to extend a supporting hand to Lady Adelaide. Foolish Lady Adelaide, recognizing Mary as the person who had most likely banged that service door against her bottom, slapped Mary's hand away, scowling fiercely.

The result of that unfortunate bit of temper was that, after teetering for a long horrible moment, trying to right herself, Lady Adelaide entirely lost her battle for balance and slipped down the stairs.

As she realized her peril, Lady Adelaide belatedly reached out toward Mary, but succeeded only in pulling poor Mary down after her, tea tray and cups and saucers and utensils and silver tea service and all. Lady Adelaide fairly sailed down the staircase in a most undignified way, just as if sledding in winter, Mary tumbled after her fallen ladyship just like Jack after Jill, and it was a great miracle, according to some of the servants who were now arriving from all corners of the house to find out what all the commotion was about, that neither girl was scalded by the hot water nor concussed by hitting heads against the stairs.

The two young ladies came separately to rest at the bottom of the landing. When the tumble had done, anyone could see that Lady Adelaide's fine new dress was ruined:

she was lying in an angry, undignified heap on her back in the vestibule hallway covered in milk, broken china, and little sticky crumb-cakes. She was so obviously angry that, for a moment, the other servants who had come to assist hesitated to approach her.

Lady Adelaide shrieked at Mary in most unladylike tones, "Wretched girl! You struck me with that door! On purpose! See what mischief you've done!"

At this juncture, the Duke of Sarratt's deep, faintly amused voice could be heard as he approached the scene of chaos from his personal library above. Mary, very embarrassed, brushed herself off and cowered at the corner of the staircase, beginning to pick up the mess. A footman began to help her, and one of the maids, screwing her courage to the sticking place, went to assist the livid Lady Adelaide.

His grace called out, "Adelaide, my dear—calm yourself! Who struck whom? Who struck whom where? And, pray, with what?"

Lady Adelaide, aware that the duke had not yet seen the full extent of the accident, flushed full red, as she had not at all intended to give his grace such a glimpse of her termagant nature. She gasped with regret, and sputtered again, looking for an answer to give his grace to explain her lapse in conduct.

Feeling humiliated to be found in such disarray by the man she intended would marry her, and really made even more angry by his having overhead her screaming like a fishwife, she felt she must find an object for blame other than herself. A servant always being, from her point of view, a suitable target for wrath, she decided to scapegoat poor Mary.

"Duke! Pray, come, lend me a hand!" said Lady Adelaide in a tone of outraged innocence and injury. "It is beyond all things—this horrid maid of yours has struck me!"

"Struck you? Surely not," he cried as he rounded the last landing. "Do you say the girl was lying in wait for you?"

"I did not say precisely that she lay in wait for me. I said she struck me. With a door," she added in helpful explanation.

"Took it off the hinges and struck you? Shouldn't think a girl could do that, Adelaide."

"No, Charles. *That* door, the servants' door; this one, in the wainscoting."

"Oh, *that* door: that's the one that sticks. Not the girl's fault then—everyone knows about that silly door. I used to play hide and seek there when I was a child. I see it all now—door popped open and gave you a good slap, did it? My condolences, Adelaide, but you must see that it couldn't be helped."

"No, Charles, you do not understand me. I believe that the wretched chit did it on purpose—and she struck me a heavy blow, I tell you."

"On purpose? Not possible. No one can control that door, Adelaide, and no one can see from within who's approaching from without. I assure you it was an accident, and not the first one. I'm sorry it happened—it must have given you a good fright, and your frock looks in sad shape, doesn't it? What a pity."

The reminder of the unbecoming condition in which he had found her only served to raise her ire once again.

"It was *not* an accident, I tell you. Look at me! What a sight I am! I must go back home at once, my visit is ruined. Charles, I insist that that chit must be made to pay for my dress, and I'll settle for nothing less."

"Adelaide, be reasonable."

"I *am* being reasonable, Charles. I am always reasonable. Paying for breakage is our custom at home: when a servant breaks something, or ruins something, it is deducted from their wages until the item has been paid for in full. Don't you do that here?"

"No, I don't believe we do. Mother would know more precisely about such arrangements."

"It is a basic principle of domestic economy. It teaches the servants to be just as careful of one's possessions as they would be of their own—if they had any, which of course they don't, because they are servants, and so own nothing. Nothing to *speak* of, that is, beyond their little gewgaws and socks and suchlike, or whatever it is that they have, which I'm sure I don't care a fig about."

"Pardon?"

"The point is, Duke, that one *cannot* have care-for-nothing servants running rampant about one's home, acting in whatever manner they see fit, and destroying what is precious simply because they think they can get away with it, scot-free. It is a critically important economic principle, I tell you."

An unaccustomed darkness passed over the duke's features, and Lady Adelaide wondered if she had gone too far. She wondered why this might be so, for certainly the theory of servant management that she had just explained was just the same as her mother had explained to her, and to her mother before her. Still, she was taken aback when he replied, with asperity, "Adelaide, you're being unreasonable: that dress of yours cost a hundred pounds if it cost a penny."

"Indeed it did. What is that to say to the matter?"

"Do you really expect an under-housemaid to pay for your dress from her wages? It would likely take her years and years to accomplish."

"I don't care. She is insolent."

"She is not, Adelaide. She hasn't said a word. Which one was it, anyway?"

"That one," said Lady Adelaide, gesturing toward a figure in a dark dress, still picking up crumbs and pieces of plates. "I shall take the liberty of going up to Diana's room, to try to repair myself, and call for my carriage to return home. I hope I may trust you to take care of this matter on my behalf?"

"Certainly. You may be sure that I shall."

"As I am hardly in a position to remain for tea, I will call again on your mother at a more convenient time. Good-day."

"Good-day, then, Adelaide."

"Shall you be coming to the Kensley's this evening?"

"I regret not. I have business I must attend to concerning Broadbrooke."

"What a shame. Can't you leave the running of your estates to your man of business? It will be a most diverting evening, I assure you."

"It is both my duty and my desire to spend time seeing to the well-being of my tenants."

"Oh! To be sure! I did not mean at all to interfere, of course."

"I'll see you very soon."

Lady Adelaide, displeased, gave a false trill of laughter.

"Why, of course, you will! Farewell, sir."

With Lady Adelaide on her way upstairs to make her repairs, the duke turned his attention at last toward his miscreant housemaid. He walked down a few steps toward where she was still at work, just beyond sight.

His jaw dropped and his dark eyes widened. Immediately, he recognized the goddess he had first beheld in the misty lamplight a fortnight before, the same girl that he had deemed a figment of his wild imagination. Yes, it was she.

He felt his heart leap in his breast, a very odd sensation, and one he had never felt before, save on that first sight of her. Immediately he was moved to go to her, to speak to her, to induce her to speak to him.

He wanted to know everything there was to know about her—where had she come from? Why was such a paragon of grace and beauty dressed in an old round-dress, working on her hands and knees, picking up sharp shards and sticky pieces of cake and sugar?

But his grace was unable to pursue these interesting topics in any way whatsoever.

Not far from them were two footmen, a housemaid, and, of course, they were still within earshot of Lady Adelaide, his not-quite-chosen bride, who was proceeding to his ward's room to repair herself.

With the greatest reluctance, he suppressed his personal desires and confined his questions to the most obvious.

"I believe you must have fallen, too. Are you sure you are perfectly all right?"

Mary had seen the duke before, but still, she was unprepared for the physical reaction that occurred when his grace came over to her and addressed her directly. A shocking blush suffused her perfect features, causing her to stammer prettily, and stare down at the floor in confusion. She found her hands trembling, and there seemed to be a knot, or a quiver, in the pit of her stomach.

She rose to her feet, and with difficulty whispered to him, "I'm fine, sir. Thank you so much. So clumsy of me. I'm most terribly sorry."

Her heart beating like the wings of a bird, she dropped a curtsey to his grace, and then dared to look up at him again. Her eyes met his in a searching glance, curious, mesmerized, until each one of them, suddenly self-conscious, looked quickly down and away, and withdrew.

There was a moment's awkwardness between them,

broken by Mary's plaintive question, "Must I really pay for her ladyship's dress, then, your grace, as her ladyship mentioned?"

"Her dress? Whose dress? Oh, you mean that of Lady Adelaide?"

"Yes, your grace."

"No. Certainly not. Not your fault. In the heat of the moment, her ladyship was overset. It was an accident; you owe her nothing."

"Then, I suppose I must go. Have I your permission to go, your grace?"

"Go? Where?" replied the duke, with uncharacteristic obtuseness. "Why?"

"Backstairs. Please, sir. My clothes are also very dirty, and rather wet. And I'm really quite ashamed of myself."

This recital brought his grace of Sarratt back to his senses.

"No need to be ashamed—it was an accident. Of course, you may go."

She curtseyed again, keeping her eyes well averted from his.

"One moment."

"Yes, your grace?"

"You're rather well-spoken for a housemaid, are you not?"

Lady Mary Hamilton's heart began to beat fast, this time from fear of being found out, rather than from passion. She searched her mind for a plausible answer.

"Am I, sir? I suppose so."

"Why, may I ask? It is most unusual."

"Oh! If so, it must be because—my father taught me," she murmured, with desperate invention. "My papa was a deacon. In a poor country town. There were so very many of us children, and he had intended to see to it that my mother and I had all the advantages that life can provide, but then he fell ill, and then he died suddenly, and then my mother fell ill, and then she died ... the family fell upon very hard times, your grace," she explained, an answer which was, really, close enough to the truth that tears formed in Lady Mary's dark violet eyes.

Moved by this recital, the duke was hard pressed to find a suitable reply.

"I see. How very unfortunate."

"Yes, sir; it was, sir. Will that be all?"

"For now. You may go."

She was such a lovely, even rather refined creature; what a pity that her family had had to send the child into service.

As the duke watched the girl with the violet eyes disappear behind the door again, leaving his presence, he was prey to the oddest sensation of regret. From that night on, the new housemaid Mary appeared to the duke in passionate dreams he mentioned to no one, but kept locked away in his heart.

Chapter 7

When Lady Mary arrived down at the housekeepers' room, she was very nervous, afraid that everyone back-stairs would bite her head off for having dropped the tray, and ruined the tea set. She entered the back hall carrying the broken pieces of china, threw them in a bin, and was ready to take brushes and clothes out to the hall again to finish the job, when Mrs. Brindle told her it had already been taken care of, and not to worry.

Not to worry? What a surprise when Mary discovered that, although the servants' hall was abuzz with the dramatic story of the tray and the tumbling falls, all their sympathy was for herself, with none for Lady Adelaide, who, it seemed, was no favorite with the staff.

Even Mrs. Brindle turned out to be a source of consolation, and not censure, saying to Lady Mary, patting her on the hand, "Never you mind, girl. These things happen. That door has been a trouble to the servants of this house since the silly thing was built, and all the quality here know it. His grace didn't scold you, did he?"

"No, Mrs. Brindle, not at all."

"The family knows all about it. Used to play in there when they were young. Nor would her grace scold you for such a thing, or Miss Diana. They're real quality, not the top-lofty sort, like that Lady Adelaide."

"A sour apple, she is, if you asks me," interjected Thomas, the third footman.

"There's no need to be talking in that impertinent way about her ladyship, I'm sure, Thomas, even if it is the Lord's solemn gospel truth," said Mrs. Brindle, her eyes twinkling. This comment, coming from the usually starchy Mrs. Brindle, had all the servants present in whoops.

One of the girls whispered to Mary, "It's no secret in this house that no one downstairs can abide Lady Adelaide. We'll be in for a rough ride if his grace takes it into his head to marry her."

"They are engaged, then?" asked Mary, feeling the flutter in her heart again.

"Not quite. But it is a likely match."

Another girl interjected, "Boswell, the duke's man, told me straight out just the other day he don't think the duke is going to marry, not ever at all."

"Yes, he will. His mother won't let him stay a bachelor. I've heard them talking. She wants a grandchild in the worst way, and don't care if she has to bring Lady Adelaide into the house in order to do it."

"Nonsense, Meg. Her grace wants her son to marry, but she don't prefer Lady Adelaide; I've heard her say as much."

"The trouble is, his grace has taken it into his head that she's someone he can live with as a matter of convenience; I heard him say that once, and that he'll just have to get used to her.

"Don't see how his grace could live with her ladyship.

He's not cork-brained, and that's what a man'd have to be to live with her.

"No, his grace is one of those hard-nosed permanent bachelor types. He's not fit to be married," opined Grace Marten. "Not to anyone, really."

"That's the truth of it. He prefers his books, his newspapers, his horses, his tenants, his politics, and his hard bout at Jackson's," said Thomas, with undisguised admiration.

"He'll have to marry someone, or the estates will go to that cousin of his. He won't be able to look after them half as well, so it's best if the duke settles down and has his own heir to leave things to."

"But why pick that woman? That brother of hers is a wastrel, and he wants to get his hands on the Sarratt estates."

"The duke won't let him. He'll pay off his gambling debts, if the two of them get engaged, but he'll not let the bloke squeeze another penny out of him. Make him go off to the Continent instead, I should think."

At this Mrs. Brindle said it was time to call it quits.

She told everyone in the hall that they were to stop right now, thank you, now that they had had a good gossip about the quality, which, she reminded them with a grin, was entirely against the rules, and would not be countenanced.

"Her grace has rung for tea," said Mrs. Brindle. "Will you take it up to her, Mary?"

Mary's gorgeous eyes widened.

"Are you sure you trust me to take it up, especially after the mull I made of it this morning?"

"I'm sure you won't be dumping the tray in her grace's lap, dearie. Don't use that tricky door if you're worried about it. Just go through the other corridor. Change your apron, and up you go, don't take all day about it."

As Mrs. Brindle watched the new housemaid taking

the tray upstairs, she allowed herself to wonder a little. Where *had* Buckley found that girl? She was such a beauty—Mrs. Brindle had had to hand out scoldings right and left to male staff who were plotting excuses to talk to her. Mary didn't seem to be much of a flirt, which was a blessing, and she seemed not the least bit flighty.

However, there was certainly something smoky, something that was just a bit hard to put one's finger on. What was it? Mary was a little old to have just started in service, and she was very inexperienced, considering her age. What was she, twenty? By that time, most girls would already have been working for five years or more—what had she been doing in her youth? Where precisely had she come from? Why was she so well-spoken? Who had schooled her?

These were issues that cried out to be addressed, but Mrs. Brindle knew she had not the time, as she had set herself the onerous task today of finally settling the household accounts. She put it in the back of her mind that she would question Buckley about her, first chance she got.

Mary scratched at the door of the dowager's sittingroom, and was admitted. Holding the silver tray as steadily as she could, Mary opened the door by backing in, and then turned around; she almost dropped the tray again.

Somehow she had expected to see a huge whale of a woman, an imposing figure in a high turban dressed in odd colors.

But here she was faced with a small, silvery creature working on an embroidery so fine as to defy description, a woman with a pretty laugh as musical as a waterfall. As soon as Mary set eyes on her, she knew she liked the dowager. She had still-sparkling blue eyes, framed by the wrinkles that occur from years of sweet smiles and laughter, and with a halo of white hair.

The dowager duchess motioned her to set the tray down, and was about to dismiss her, but then she leaned over on her polished wooden cane, saying, "Who's this? It's not Helen, is it? Come here farther into the light so I can see your face, my dear; my eyes aren't what they used to be. No, I don't believe we've met."

"No, ma'am, we haven't met," said Mary, dropping her a curtsey. "I'm . . . I'm Mary."

"Mary, is it? A pretty name. I hope you enjoy your work with us, Mary."

"Thank you, your grace," she said with another curtsey. "I'm sure I shall."

Her grace smiled politely and returned to her embroidery. Mary began setting out the tea service in its entirety. She was careful, as Mrs. Brindle had taught her, not to let the pieces of silverware touch each other, for they might clank. The same danger existed for the china teacups and saucers and plates—each one had to be handled separately, for if any one was damaged, the entire set was ruined. Working as carefully as she might, she set out the plate that was piled high with delicious little teacakes; a glance at them made her mouth water. She thought for a moment of the time when just such a delectable assortment of sweets had been set out for herself: it seemed like a lifetime ago, and so it was.

She was just setting out the last napkin when the side entrance to her grace's sitting-room burst open, and a gangly girl rushed into the room, and thrust her dark-blonde head into the duchess's lap, and began to weep in loud, angry sobs.

"Oh, Nana!" the girl cried, "I cannot bear it!"

"Diana!" said the duchess. "Try to calm yourself, child. What can be the matter?"

"Nana, it's that horrid Henchart person!"

"You mustn't refer to Lady Adelaide in that way, Diana. It's not done."

"I'm sorry, Nana, but she says the most horrid things to me, every time she sees me, she lords it over me, just as if she were my mother or something, and I can't bear it anymore, I tell you! It's just beyond anything!"

"Tell me exactly what happened. What did she do?"

"She—she fairly *pushed* her way into my room, on the pretext of having soiled her dress or some silly story, and while she was there, preening herself and putting herself back together, she just started talking at me and talking at me until I could bear it no longer!"

"What did she say?"

"Well, first, in that horrid patronizing way of hers, she rattled on to me about *everything* in the world having to do with polite society, just as if I weren't already out, which I am, and about how to cut a dash in society, and she just went on, and on, and on."

"I don't precisely understand: you are upset because Lady Adelaide's stories about society bored you to tears?"

"No, Nana, no! It wasn't precisely what she said; it was more the awful, snide, knowing *way* she talked to me! All about how much trouble I seemed to be having in my first season, and how I'm not taking at all, and it made me a complete ugly fool and it was awful. She went on about how *one* mistake made in view of the patronesses at Almack's would be enough to taint my whole season, and how I'd better just watch my step, and listen to her advice, and follow it or it would be the worse for me.

"She talked about everybody's high expectations of me as to marriage, and how very rich I am, and how gawky and thin and sallow I am, and how I must be rather a disappointment to you and to Uncle Charles, and how I'll never make a decent marriage even though I *am* rich as Croesus, and what a great pity it is that it should be so.

"Lady Adelaide even brought up that story about my coming out of the Queen's drawing room, having turned away from the Queen first, which is of course complete rubbish, and she wasn't even there, so how does she know what I did?"

"Precisely."

"Then, she began talking about my unfortunate looks. She mentioned how green doesn't suit my complexion, and yellow doesn't suit it, and pink makes me look faded, and however I am going to find a color suitable to be presented in at court, she just can't imagine! And to find a color that would suit me at my come-out ball, well, she says, she just feels very sorry for you, Nana, because you are advanced in years, and shouldn't have to carry such a burden."

"She referred to me as 'advanced in years,' did she?" asked the dowager, with a sudden loss of humor.

"Yes, she did!"

"I see," said the duchess, with no hint of forgiveness.

"And, Nana, Lady Adelaide just kept on and on, insulting me at every opportunity in that awful, sneaking underhanded way of hers."

"Oh, dear."

"I'm just beside myself. I don't know how I can ever think to meet her again. It was always the same: on the outside she was all honeyed smiles and sweetness, as if seeming to be giving me good advice, but underneath, she was just making me feel small, and ugly, and hopeless, and Nana, I just can't bear it. I can't stand the woman. If Uncle Charles marries her, and I have to live with that woman under the same roof, I shan't put up with it, not for all the love I bear you and not for all the love I bear Uncle Charles.''

''There's no need to speak in extremes, Diana.''

''It is an extreme matter, Nana! If I have to hear that woman criticizing me one more minute, I shall kill myself, I swear it.''

''I won't hear any such talk, Diana.''

''Or I'll kill *her!*''

''That will do, Diana! This outburst of intemperateness is at an end, I tell you, from this moment on. I am sympathetic to your feelings if Lady Adelaide was unkind to you, but I will not endure your lowering yourself to making threats and having tantrums.''

''Why does he have to marry *her?* You don't like her, do you? If you tell me she's 'perfectly amiable,' I'll laugh out loud, for you know full well that's a hum.''

''Don't say 'hum,' dear. It's undignified.''

'' 'My poor Diana,' she said to me. 'Isn't it a *shame* the way the sunlight brings out the freckles in your complexion? Makes you look quite brown, doesn't it?' Ooh, I could have pulled out her hair when she told me that.''

''I'm sure she didn't *mean* to be unkind.''

''Oh, she's *always* unkind. I don't know whether she *means* to be or not, but I think she knows no alternative. Nana, I'm in despair. Must Lady Adelaide be the one to shepherd me through the season? That's what she means to do, I'm sure of it. That's what Uncle Charles means her to do, too, doesn't he? Can't you do it?''

''My dear, I hope you know that I'd far prefer to be there with you myself, but my stamina will not permit me to endure the endless bout of balls and routs and staying up till dawn and the rest of it.''

''If you can't, can't Uncle Charles do so?''

''Charles's social stamina is excellent, as is his taste, but he really has not the patience to accompany you, either. And in particular, there is woman's work to be done: shopping day after day—we've still not purchased your entire wardrobe. Charles has not the patience, much less the interest, to fuss over one shade of muslin versus another, and frills versus ruching, and determining precisely which style of dress befits you best. I don't think he could do the job well at all. It is far better to have a female nearer your own age involved in that extremely crucial enterprise."

"Perhaps so, but, please, not Lady Adelaide!"

"Diana, Diana, we must make do with whichever possibilities life presents us, mustn't we? I find all this conflict most distressing. I am getting a headache."

"Oh, I'm sorry, Nana."

"Have patience with Lady Adelaide. I am sure she means well."

"All right, Nana," said Diana reluctantly.

Mary, having invisibly finished her tasks, was engaged in quietly creeping out of the room, when Diana's eye lit up upon her.

"Who's that girl, Nana?"

"She's new. Her name is Mary."

"She's very pretty," said Diana, continuing to speak of her just as if she weren't there.

"Isn't she, though? I think it's the color of her eyes— almost a dark shade of lavender. Not just in the common way, to be sure. In fact, her features strongly remind me of something, or someone, but I can't for the life of me think who or what; I suppose this is further proof of my advancing years. Is it a figure in a painting that she resembles, perhaps? Something by Vermeer, or perhaps Botticelli? Mary, come over here. This is Miss Leigh, my son's ward."

Taken unaware, Mary looked up, stopped what she was doing, and strode elegantly over to them. She extended her hand civilly, smiled, and said, "How do you do, Miss Leigh. I am so pleased to make your acquaintance."

Diana Leigh stared at her for a moment, and then exchanged a puzzled glance with the duchess.

Flushing beet red, Mary realized her error; instantly she retracted her hand, dropped a quick curtsey, and said "Miss Diana. Yes, of course. Sorry, ma'am. Sorry, miss.'

Another flush suffused Mary's face. What a numskull thing to do! How could she have forgotten herself so completely? She had managed perfectly well, all things considered, working downstairs for a fortnight, but bring her upstairs, rubbing shoulders with the quality, and she got into one dreadful mess after another. It was time to retreat, instantly, or face unmasking.

"Will there be anything else, or may I go now, ma'am?' she murmured, chagrined.

The dowager duchess looked Mary over very carefully indeed before answering, "You may go, Mary."

After she had left the room, Diana Leigh, with amazement, asked her guardian's mother, "Did you see what she did, Nana?"

"I did, indeed. Most unusual."

"Extending her hand to me, just as if she were 'to the manner born.'"

"Quite a remarkable performance."

"Performance? Why, do you think the theatrical stage may have been where she learned to behave like that' How very singular."

"I can't think of anything else that *would* account for her conduct. Come to think of it, where else *but* in the theater would a girl have learned that carriage, that elegance, and that address?"

Diana clapped her hands together and laughed with delight.

"Fancy having an actress serving as one's housemaid! I like it above all things!"

At this comment, the dowager duchess's face began to darken with disapprobation.

There were some situations at Sarratt House in which her grace would intervene when she saw that things had gone too far out of control. This was one such situation. A pretty housemaid was difficult enough—she could upset an entire household, turning footman against footman and groom against groom, turning the whole social order topsy-turvy in very short order, but this was worse. Having a lovely young woman in the house with an acknowledged theatrical background, one who had been used to behaving according to the free ways common to theatrical persons? No, that would not do. Such a person did not belong in service.

"Ring for Buckley, will you, Diana? I think he and I should have a little chat about this Mary he and Mrs. Brindle have engaged."

"Why, Nana? She seems nice enough. Please don't let her go just because she tried to shake my hand."

"Well, my dear, perhaps the girl's manners are a bit too free to be suitable for work as a housemaid."

"How can that be?"

"Diana," she said in a warning tone, "It is a matter of the influence she has on the tone of our home. You are not too young to learn that, in domestic matters, one can never be too careful about the quality and character of the persons one admits into one's household."

"Oh!" said Diana, suddenly realizing the dowager's objection. "To be sure."

"The matter is by no means decided in any case. On the surface, Mary seems most suitable. I will leave the final decision up to him. It is merely that it is Buckley's duty to make sure that all our staff, upon whom we depend, and who have access to our very homes, are worthy of the trust we repose in them. I shall ask that he question the girl with particular care as to her background, and to dismiss her unless he can satisfy himself that what appears to be the case, is in fact the case.''

''Yes, Nana. I hope she stays.''

''So do I, dear, but we shall know what must be done about her by the afternoon. It's always best to be careful about one's retainers.''

''Yes, Nana. Of course.''

Chapter 8

Having finished serving the Dowager Duchess of Sarratt, blissfully unaware that, as a result of that episode, her own character would soon be the subject of investigation, Lady Mary Hamilton brought the serving tray downstairs again, and was soon set to other tasks. She spent what she thought was an inordinate amount of time taking tissue paper to some silk damask wall coverings, trying to lift the dirt from them.

Lady Mary actually got her ears boxed shortly thereafter by her nemesis, Susan Bowker, for the heinous crime of failing to properly remove the tarnish from the most intricate sections of the second-best set of silver plate; the silverware had a curled rose and leaf pattern that was cut deeply into the metal, and, as a result, each piece was both precious and almost impossible to clean.

Mr. Buckley, meanwhile, had been called in to meet with the dowager duchess; after the episode had been explained to him, he was quick to carry out her request that he interview the girl. He waited for a suitable moment to occur, toward the middle of the afternoon, a quiet time when he might call Mary into his room and question her in private.

When, in response to his summons, she arrived in his small office room, she was very obviously nervous; all the staff knew that they were in for a scold when Buckley called to speak with them individually.

Initially, Lady Mary was most afraid Mr. Buckley would ask her for money to pay for Lady Adelaide's ruined dress, and for the china tea service. But his very first words belied this.

"Tell me, just who are you, my girl?" he demanded in a rough and angry voice.

"Why, you know who I am. I'm Mary Simpson, Mr. Buckley. Is that what you meant?"

"Mary Simpson. Cousin to Mrs. Fanny Simpson, Fanny being an acquaintance of my cousin Fred Wartle, which is how you came to us for this position."

"Yes, sir. Fanny Simpson arranged it. Is my work not satisfactory?"

"Your work is satisfactory; your manners are in question. You acted above your station recently when you were upstairs. Show me your hands."

She did so.

Afraid she was about to be turned out onto the street, her white hands were shaking.

"Now, tell me—why are you shaking? Just why are you so frightened, Mary? Is there something about you that you haven't told us?"

"N-no, sir," said Mary, sounding not at all convincing.

"Look at your hands."

"What about them?"

"They're rubbed raw."

"Y-yes, sir. All the cleaning, you know."

"You told us you were from the country, didn't you?"

"Y-yes, sir."

"Country girls don't have fine hands like yours."

"Begging your pardon, my hands aren't fine, as you can see. They're covered with blisters."

"Don't take me for a flat, Mary. They're blistered because these hands have never, ever known hard work. What I must know is this—just what kind of work *have* these little hands known?"

"What do you mean, Mr. Buckley?"

"I think you know perfectly well what I mean. You displayed manners far above your station to her grace and Miss Diana. Your hands as well are unsuited to your station. A glance at them suggests that, prior to your employment in this household, those hands of yours have been habitually swathed in gloves. This tells me that you have obviously lied about where you've come from, and what work you've done. You speak in a manner far above your station, you're much too pretty, and you carry yourself too well. Explain all of that to me, if you can."

"I-I . . ."

"I can easily consult the London Registry, with whom you are said to be listed, though I have my doubts about it now. Shall I do that?"

"As you like, sir."

"Shall I just come to the point, and tell you straight out what I believe your last line of work was? I think it was in the theater."

"No, sir!" said Lady Mary, genuinely shocked. "I wouldn't do that. Never!"

"If not the theater, then I suggest you are a member of a notorious profession that is even lower than that of an actress. What is your reply?"

At this, Mary gasped, and blushed from the roots of her hair to her cheeks, till she was a shade of apple-red, and said nothing.

"I am very disappointed in you, Mary, and in Fanny Simpson, who was so foolish as to vouch for your character. I don't know how you had the temerity to think that you could pass yourself off as a respectable girl. The next time you seek out a fat pigeon to pluck, you'd better find a victim whose retainers have no respect for him, and who are willing to assist you in your plan to cozen your way into a rich man's arms. What is the world coming to, that a light-skirt has the audacity to try to invade a noble household in order to insinuate herself into a nobleman's heart!

"Throwing yourself deliberately in the way of his grace, thinking to make one of his stable of ladybirds! Well, you have missed your mark by a long chalk, girl! His grace of Sarratt ain't that kind of man!

"Did you really think we would all stand by and watch you run tame in the household and act out your various intrigues without stopping you? Famous it would be if we were so neglectful of our duty! Now, pack your things at once, and be off, doxy! You know just where you belong!"

Throughout this harangue, Lady Mary's face had alternately reddened and whitened; by its end, she was shaking with rage, and could no longer contain herself.

"Silence! How dare you speak to me in such a way!" she thundered imperiously. "How dare you have the insolence to cast aspersions on my character! I have done nothing whatever to merit such, I do not scruple to say, egregious mistreatment at your hands!"

Mr. Buckley turned and faced the girl full on, and did so with renewed interest. A small smile played upon his lips, for he realized that he had won his three-way wager with Mrs. Brindle and her grace the dowager duchess. This was going to be an enlightening speech, he felt sure. He let the girl continue, enjoying himself immensely.

"I had an accident on the landing, Mr. Buckley. That is the worst of what I have done. If I must pay for that dress and the tea set, I shall make arrangements to do so; I am sorry that I tried to shake Miss Leigh's hand. Those are the crimes you may honestly lay at my door, but the rest of what you have said is due to sheer prejudice!

"I never pretended to have been experienced as a maid, and these hands attest to the honesty of my statement. I claimed to have been recommended for this position by Fanny Simpson, and indeed I was! In terms of the work I have done here at Sarratt House, from the very night I arrived, I have done my best to keep up with the, may I say, extortionate and prejudicially unfair demands of your staff upon me! I wish I might box *your* ears as soundly as your staff have boxed *mine!*

"Although I have borne all this in noble silence, you now attempt to besmirch my honesty and my character, baselessly. *That* is the outside of enough!"

Hot tears of rage began to fill Lady Mary's eyes. She knew not who would shelter her, but her pride could bear no more such mistreatment, and she turned to take herself up to her room to pack her belongings.

"I shall be pleased to take my leave of you, sir, at once!" she flung at him, incensed.

Mr. Buckley put a hand to her shoulder to stop her; she turned around, trying in her rage to cast his arm off her, and found to her dismay that the man was actually smiling broadly at her.

"What are you smiling at? How dare you answer my accusations with derision!"

"I beg your pardon, ma'am," said the steward, sketching her a bow.

"Are you quite mad?" said his unmollified victim, still regarding him with the deepest possible suspicion.

"Please try to understand that her grace, upon your

conversing with Miss Diana today, immediately perceived you were not of the working class. Her grace then directed me to determine your correct social provenance. When you entered this room just now, I myself inspected you closely, and I perceived the truth of the dowager's judgment. Your hair, your nails, your hands, your manner, your carriage, your address, your tone of voice all militated against your belonging to that yeoman class which generally enters into service.

"It was by no means unreasonable for me to question you, in order to determine whether your manner and carriage were due to having had other origins in other worlds. These other circumstances most probably would be in either the theater, or in the—how shall I put it?—the Cyprian set.

"The third, and least likely possibility, of course, was that you are actually a person of genteel birth, who must have fallen on hard times."

Lady Mary, still very angry, stared at him in stony silence, her violet eyes flashing.

"I must beg your forgiveness for my having had so rudely to badger you into revealing yourself as you truly are, but I point out to you that you made no effort whatsoever to be frank with me, much less to enlighten me as to your true situation.

"Your language just now and your conduct have, with the very greatest eloquence, revealed the gentility of your origins to me. That being the case, the security of the household remains inviolate; protecting the welfare of the household is, you must recall, my duty. I hope you will accept my apologies for this interlude, and return to your duties, as a valued member of the domestic staff of Sarratt House."

Lady Mary was stunned by this sudden turnabout. Her mind whirled, put quite off balance.

"Well! I hardly know what to say."

"I assure you, Mary, that no one in the household will make any attempt to determine any further details of your origins, if you do not wish them generally known."

"No, I—I do not."

"Will you stay on with us, then?"

"Yes, Mr. Buckley," she said, grateful to have a place to lay her head once more, and not to be thrust upon London all alone, lest word of her get back to her pursuers.

Chapter 9

Mary's life in service had devolved into routine; she knew what was to be done, and she did it. She knew where things belonged, and saw to it that they were put there. She knew which footmen on the staff she must never be alone with; she had befriended most of the girls, with the exception of Susan. Mrs. Brindle and Mr. Buckley had come to know her and trust her. She was biding her time, and doing quite well. Sometimes she wished she had Fanny to confide in, but for the most part she felt perfectly content.

She caught glimpses of the duke from time to time; he always favored her with a smile, and this habit pained her. He seemed to her so tall and handsome and kind; it seemed so unfair that she should meet such an excellent man under such ridiculous circumstances.

She was perfectly aware that the mere act of bringing the duke's image to mind was enough to make her breath quicken and have her blushing again.

Had she met the noble Duke of Sarratt in the course

of being properly brought out in London, in her true form, as the Lady Mary Hamilton, only daughter and sole heiress to the Earl of Hamilton, it would have been quite a different matter altogether.

Often, late at night after work, she would lean back on her cot while she allowed her mind to ramble on what might have been.

If only . . .

If only she had been properly presented at Court . . .

If only she had been properly presented to polite society . . .

If only her lady mother had lived long enough to guide her daughter through the ton's dangerous shoals . . .

If only the handsome Duke of Sarratt had first seen her dressed in an exquisite white gown by Madame Vergere, her neck and ears ornamented with the Hamilton diamonds—*then* she could have given that Lady Adelaide a run for her money! Lady Mary Hamilton would have been well able to stand up to Lady Adelaide Henchart, and stare her down if need be. Lady Mary Hamilton would not have had to suffer her insults in silence, as had happened this morning.

In her mind's eye, she pictured the proper version of things.

First of all, she would have been presented at Court, managing that funny old style of dress with the hoops, with a headdress of plumes and lace lappets—Mama would have shown her how to manage the hoops. She would have had her own come-out. She would have received vouchers to Almack's Assembly Rooms, and she would have gone there, accompanied by her parents, every Wednesday night.

Her mother would have fussed for months over which dresses were most suited to her. One night she might have chosen a white muslin dress with just a shine of rose-pink to it; something that seemed plain and demure, suitable to a girl in her first season, but one that was cut with exquisite taste and had extraordinary detailing. She would have worn the diamonds, of course; not too many of them, Mother would never have let her appear vulgar. She would have had a headdress of fresh young rosebuds, and new gloves and new slippers, and she would have practiced dancing with her papa for weeks before the event.

There she would have been, one night at Almack's, accompanied by her doting parents, Lord and Lady Hamilton, her mother so kind and so beautiful; her father so handsome and strong. She could almost see how proud they were of her being there, and how proud she was to be there with them.

That night the name of the Duke of Sarratt would have been announced. She would have turned toward the entranceway, and their eyes would have met and locked together, just as they had at their very first encounter, and just as they had this morning on the stairs, and just as they had this afternoon in his grace's library.

But at Almack's he would have approached her. He would have found some acquaintance who knew the earl and countess, and he would have asked to be introduced to them. On being introduced to them, he would have sought an introduction to their daughter.

She would have blushed just as deeply as she had on the staircase, or the library, but it would have been a blush that admitted further conversation. He would have asked for the honor of a dance, and she, of course, would have granted it. She knew that the very first time he touched her hand to lead her onto the floor, would have been enough to set her heart trembling.

After the dance, he would have brought her refreshments. They would have made fun of the insipid offerings, and the stale slices of bread and butter, the tasteless orgeat and cloying ratafia. They would have had acquaintances in common, and they would have discussed their common acquaintances; they would have spoken easily about life in London, about cultural affairs, about paintings, about theater, about the opera, and they would have laughed together and savored each other's company.

That is what would have happened, thought Lady Mary; it is what should have been.

But—such was not the case.

What really had happened was that Lady Mary had first met the duke standing on a streetcorner on a rainy night, unaccompanied, like a classic woman of easy virtue.

She had next seen the duke on a staircase landing. He was dressed in the first style of elegance, and she was wearing the faded, patched, hand-me-down dress of an under-servant. She had met him working on her knees cleaning up a mess of shard, working at his feet like the skivvy she had become, while his well-born near-betrothed sneered at her and berated her loudly in front of him.

Now, whenever she met him, it was a simple meeting: that of master and servant.

The whole thing was impossible. Even normal conversation was impossible between her and the Duke of Sarratt, between his entire class and her new class; social intercourse between them was a thing forbidden, and not without reason.

The sad fact was that by the time she left this low life behind, and assumed her true identity, the Duke of Sarratt would already be a married man, and that would be that.

For now, for so long as she must remain incognita, she was not even a person to the duke, she was just another household implement. It was as Mrs. Brindle had said—working as part of the staff in a great house, she was as a vase, or a lamp or a curtain, not an animate being.

Remembering this, her headaches would begin, night after night. Night after night she would be denied the solace of sleep, plagued by the same lowering thoughts.

There was no way out. Nothing could be helped; nothing could be changed. Whatever might have occurred between her and the Duke of Sarratt, whatever might have been had her situation been other than it was, was not worth considering.

The die was cast; Lady Mary Hamilton had no power to change what was the case.

Chapter 10

The Earl and Countess of Hamilton had been a uniquely happy and loving couple, despite the fact that one child only was born to them. It was after the earl died, from wounds sustained in a terrible carriage accident, that the lives of the widowed Countess of Hamilton and her young daughter began to change, for the worse.

Lady Mary had been only ten when her father died; her mother was all of twenty-nine. They spent a year in deepest mourning, grieving for a man of unequalled good character, depending upon one another for support and understanding.

The countess had been Lady Elizabeth Marton before her marriage; she was just sixteen, a great beauty who was the toast of London at the time the Earl of Hamilton, many years her senior, met her. He fell in love with her the moment he set eyes on her—as had many men in London that season—but she returned his regard many times over.

It was a splendid match; it was a splendid marriage

for long, wonderful years. The couple were known to be very close, very unfashionably devoted to one another. When her husband was taken from her, she was devastated. She had, by then, no other family; her husband, the earl, had been the last of his line.

It was perhaps for this reason that Elizabeth, Countess of Hamilton, had been such an easy target. Through some financial machinations, which her mother had never fully revealed to her, she had been put under obligation to one Sir Barton Ayleston, whom she had met during her period of mourning. The upshot was, she consented to become Sir Barton's wife.

Her poor mother was never the same again.

Lady Mary and her mother, now Lady Elizabeth Ayleston, were taken away from Hamilton House in London in the year 1814. Her stepfather sent them to live year-round at Danby Court, a huge stone castle in the farthest reaches of Cumberland.

It was not an entirely unhappy existence. She had her mother to herself, most of the time, for Sir Barton spent great stretches of time away on business. He would appear, every once in a while, to spend the night, but for the most part, he seemed more like an occasional visitor than a real part of Lady Mary's life.

The saddest thing about the marriage, at least from Lady Mary's point of view, was that her mother was, during those three years, generally in a delicate condition. Her husband being absolutely desperate for a male heir, Lady Elizabeth found herself perpetually increasing. None of the babies lived; most frequently the pregnancies ended early.

Her health was ruined. Lady Mary watched her poor mother slowly waste away, until, in the end, at the age of thirty-seven, she finally succumbed to childbed fever, worn out from trying to produce a son to satisfy Sir Barton.

Only young Lady Mary Hamilton was left, the last of her line. She had to continue to live with her stepfather, having no other relatives left on earth.

After her mother's death, her stepfather began to take more of an interest in her, if one can call confinement interest. Sir Barton gave particular orders which circumscribed Lady Mary's existence: she was not allowed to go about in local society. She was not allowed to go anywhere save on the extensive lands and parks belonging to Danby Court.

Sir Barton made sure his stepdaughter had the proper governesses and dancing-masters at Danby, but he never permitted her to go to Dunberton, much less London, not even when she left the schoolroom and might have been expected to have a come-out at last.

If Lady Mary had not had faithful Fanny Simpson living at Danby Court with her, she might have withered there entirely, since Sir Barton Ayleston had no love for her, nor any use for her. He was not obviously unkind to her, for he neglected her too thoroughly; beyond circumscribing her existence, he left the girl entirely to her own devices.

While she was younger, she did not mind much. The area itself was lovely, and she loved exploring its hills and lakes and waterfalls by taking long trips on horseback, accompanied by Fanny Simpson, whom she had taught to ride, and her groom, Collins.

At home, for amusement she played the harpsichord. She studied French, Italian, dancing, and she painted very nicely. She learned to dance, and to embroider, and was given the advantage of learning all of a lady's accomplishments.

But though her stepfather saw to her education, and

never begrudged her any material possessions, he did severely limit her company to members of the immediate household. She never was visited, or went visiting. She attended no balls, outings, or any other activities that a girl might. Other young ladies in the neighborhood would attend the Dunberton Assemblies; Lady Mary was not even aware of them. Kept far from any companions save family servants, it was an exceedingly lonely life for a girl.

Once, when she thought she could stand the loneliness no longer, she had put down her copy of *The Lady's Magazine,* gone bravely to her stepfather's room and begged him to grant her three wishes: to take her to London, have her presented at court, and let her enjoy a come-out, for, she told Sir Barton, she remembered living with her mama and her papa, a noisy place, full of gaiety and wonders. She also reminded Sir Barton that her mother had always promised she should have a come-out, as befitted the daughter of the Earl of Hamilton.

When she mentioned this, imploring him, Sir Barton had looked at her rather strangely, and made no direct reply, but sighed, folded his newspaper, and sent her out of the room again.

Lady Mary would always remember that odd, annoyed look on her stepfather's face, for it was the beginning of what she later referred to as the "Dark Era of Gervase."

Gervase Ayleston had arrived at Danby Court two days later, an extremely dull and uninteresting person whose personality had all the fascination of a bowl of thin gruel. For the next year (which seemed to her like a century) the dreadful man never left her side. The two young people were thrown together constantly; picnics were arranged for them, and elaborate country outings. They drove together or rode together every day, and dined together every evening. They saw each other so often that Lady

Mary developed the heartiest dislike of him in the shortest amount of time.

As if this burden were insufficient, toward the middle of her twentieth year, their attack began again, this time in earnest.

Every Sunday, Gervase Ayleston would meet her for tea, take her soft hand in his, and ask if she would do him the honor to become his bride. Every Sunday she would reply, "No, thank you, Gervase. I fear we should not suit."

Gervase never seemed particularly surprised or upset by her refusals, and nothing, it seemed could dissuade him from pressing himself forth as a suitor, again and again. As the time of her twenty-first birthday approached, the time at which control over the Hamilton estates would pass from Sir Barton to Lady Mary, Gervase became ever more insistent, and ever more obnoxious in his approach.

This was probably because, the late earl having been a liberal man, ahead of his time, he had left his estates settled entirely upon his daughter Lady Mary in default of male heirs.

She was an heiress; as such, she was fair game for Gervase. In pursuit of his prey, Gervase began to sneak about the corridors waiting for her, trying to steal a kiss or a quick embrace, which actions, of course, only made him more repellent to her.

She had told Fanny Simpson what Gervase and his uncle were trying to do; Fanny was worried sick about how to thwart their plot. It was at that time that the two women had begun making plans for Lady Mary, upon her majority, to come down to London and try to set up an establishment of her own. Fanny was sent to Dunberton, to sell some garnets her mother had given her, so she might have money in case she should suddenly require funds.

Sir Barton and Gervase must have got wind of this

transaction, for it was only two days later that Lady Mary was actually attacked.

She was just coming down for dinner, and had rounded the stairs in the southwest corridor, pulling her shawl over her as she ran down; she was late, as usual, and it was even windier in the passage than was the norm. She didn't precisely know how it occurred, but she was struck a smart blow on her head from behind; she collapsed, and swooned deeply, and knew nothing more until she awoke in a traveling carriage, a baize hood over her head, and the sound of the thundering hooves of a team of horses running at full speed, making her bruised head ache most awfully.

Through the darkness of the hood, and through the throbbing pain of her injury, she could make out the voices of Sir Barton Ayleston and Gervase. It took no genius to figure out what they were doing: they had abducted her, and were bent on carrying her off to Gretna. It being already dark, they needed only that she be seen spending a single night at a public inn in the company of Gervase, sans chaperone, in order to sully her reputation. After that, marriage to Gervase would be the only possibility open to her.

With or without marriage, having been seen with Gervase at an inn overnight, she would be compromised, regardless of her own conduct or wishes. To be an heiress without a protector was no easy life.

She had managed to escape, but it had been a near thing. She had gotten away by the flimsiest of margins— a serving maid who knew of a back staircase in an inn; a cart-boy with his cart filled with straw, who thought it great fun that a real lady should want to hide in it, dirty herself and her fine clothes, and even pay him for the opportunity!

She had fled back to Fanny Simpson, and they had left

at once for London, making their plans into reality. Lady Mary knew full well that she was not out of the soup yet, not by a long chalk.

It was not enough to have once escaped from them, but she must keep firm until she had come into her majority. Then, her stepfather and his nephew would be able to do her no more harm.

Chapter 11

His grace, Charles Wellesford, Duke of Sarratt, emerged from his carriage just outside Lord Rutherfurd's townhouse on Russell Square. He was wearing biscuit-colored pantaloons, a teal green coat, cut as if to show his fighter's figure to best advantage, an off-white waist-coat, and a snow-white cravat, tied in a high and intricate knot. His grace was, without doubt, a powerful figure of a man, looking the perfect Corinthian as he stood there fingering his quizzing-glass.

The porter, peering through the glass at the sides of the front door, wondered why his grace had not yet taken the few steps up to the entranceway. His grace was, if not quite pacing back and forth on the sidewalk, certainly hesitant to enter, almost seeming to be entrapped by equal conflicting forces: one impelling him to enter, and one to flee.

The porter saw the duke take a deep breath, step manfully up to the door, and use the knocker. The door was instantly opened to admit his grace, who asked after Lady Adelaide, and was shown upstairs to the parlor.

Lady Adelaide had already spent the whole morning and early afternoon driving her abigail to distraction while choosing what to wear for this much-anticipated visit. Her ladyship had arranged herself casually upon a sofa, taking the greatest pains to appear to best advantage. Her very becoming shawl of Norwich silk had been arranged and rearranged to flow over that sofa, in what she hoped was an attractive way. Her abigail, sick of the whole business, hoped never to see that shawl again.

His grace was announced, Lady Adelaide favored him with a becoming smile, and held out her hand to him.

"Why, Duke!" said Lady Adelaide. "What a surprise!"

His grace, knowing this to be utter nonsense, approached the woman anyway. He brought her hand to his lips, and gave it a respectful kiss.

"Do be seated. Tell me, how is your family? How is your mother? How is your little ward?"

"My mother and my ward are well, thank you."

Silence fell hard upon the parlor, a silence that seemed to go on endlessly.

After some minutes, the duke spoke.

"How are your excellent parents?"

"They are very well, thank you," she said with a prim smile.

There was another awkward pause, after which the duke inquired, "How is your excellent brother, Lord Stone?"

"He is well, thank you."

The two persons stared at the floor for a while; then they each stared in opposite directions, apparently studying the ornamentation of the room.

A slight gleam appeared in the duke's eyes.

"How is your most excellent brother, Roger?" the duke added disingenuously.

Lady Adelaide herself was trying hard to stay in control, and was wondering if the Duke of Sarratt was actually baiting her, for so it seemed. Did the wretched man already know about Roger? How many others knew, if he did?

The duke, on his part, was wishing that Lady Adelaide would do something really refreshingly unexpected, such as to candidly reveal to him the truth about Roger. Her foolish, selfish, heedless brother Roger had wagered a small fortune on a race between two weasels to very bad effect, and had been forced to resort to the cents per cent again to pay his astonishing debt. The duke was certain that usurers must hold notes of hand on most of the disposable wealth of the Rutherfurd family.

It was rather a pity it had worked out that way. Always best to leave things such that persons with tendencies to profligacy were prevented from wagering away the family fortune, but it was sadly common that families would find some way to raise the blunt, in order that their sons not be clapped into prison.

"Roger is doing excellently well, thank you," said Lady Adelaide with a false smile. It would not do for the duke to know of the tribulations Roger had put them to, much less how desperate her father was for her to make this marriage at once. In an interview just this morning, he had screamed at her that it was her duty to her family to bring this man immediately up to scratch—no matter what means she had to use to do it.

Lady Adelaide had been a little unsure as to what her father had meant. Was she supposed to draw him into compromising her? How was she to accomplish that on a twenty-minute afternoon visit, pray tell?

Lady Adelaide patted the seat next to her on the sofa, indicating for him to join her, and pulled back the Norwich shawl.

The duke reluctantly moved forward and sat down. He

wondered if she expected him to take her hand. He was beginning to feel physically ill.

"Our families have known each other for these ages, have they not?" she asked.

"Yes," replied his grace blankly. "They have."

There was silence again for a moment.

Catching a look of desperation on Lady Adelaide's face, the Duke of Sarratt began actually to feel sorry for the girl. Surely, if her family hadn't been in such bad financial straits, Lady Adelaide would not have had to put herself out on the marriage block for sale to the highest bidder, which was, in this case, himself.

He began to wonder, idly, whether he ought to be in love with Lady Adelaide before he married her. Then he wondered what love really is: how could one tell if one was in love? The feelings he had in the presence of Lady Adelaide were not love, he felt sure of that. Could such feelings be cultivated by force of will? Should he try to cultivate a loving attitude toward Lady Adelaide?

Those romantic sensations he felt in the presence of that girl Mary, could they be called love? What was the meaning of those passionate dreams? Would they last? Were they real? Were they mere signs of desire?

As he was lost in this train of thought, almost before he was aware of it, these wistful words had escaped his lips: "Lady Adelaide, tell me this: do you believe in romantic love?"

She gave him a look as if he had dropped a serpent in her lap.

"Certainly not!" she exclaimed with firmness. "I hope you know, your grace, that my parents, and my mother in particular, were very strict with my upbringing; they taught me very well that persons of our class do not enter into any such common liaisons . . . by which I mean those of the 'heart.'

"To a Henchart, the very thought of romance is an unspeakable vulgarity," she said with some satisfaction.

"Quite so," the duke agreed, lamely.

It was perhaps at this juncture that it came to him in a blinding flash that a loveless marriage, rather than being a tolerable fate, was something devoutly to be avoided. He wondered what, of all things, he was going to do about it. Could he ever come to love this woman? Could this woman ever come to love him?

Would he ever feel toward Lady Adelaide the thrill he had experienced that night outside the front entrance of Sarratt House? Would he ever feel with her the excitement that was his *whenever* he was in the presence of Mary?

What did it mean? Unaccustomed as he was to topics such as love, and passion, and emotion, he felt confused and rather depressed.

His spirits now very much lowered, the duke allowed Lady Adelaide to chatter away about whatever she could, while she tried to show him she was at once knowing, flirtatious, and amusing.

He thought her laughter had begun to assume a desperate and shrill note.

He wished she would stop talking.

After the requisite time had run out, she finally did stop. Her constant attempts to flatter and entertain him had left his grace of Sarratt with a most remarkable headache.

They shook hands, and promised to encounter one another at the earliest possible opportunity.

Breathing a great sigh of relief, he bowed himself out, retrieved his curly beaver and cane, and told his coachman to convey him home. There, he changed clothes, snapped at his valet in an uncharacteristic fashion, and went out again to take refuge at his club.

"What's got into you, Sarratt?" asked the Hon. Lionel Fitzmartin as he watched his friend down two glasses of port wine in quick succession. "Looks as if you've had some bad oysters, or bad mutton, or at any event, something that's left a bad taste in your mouth. What's the matter, old man? Tell your old friend Lionel."

"Went to see Adelaide today," said the duke glumly.

"No! Don't tell me you—"

"No, I didn't. Thank god. But I meant to."

"My condolences, Sarratt. Nothing worse than trying to court a gal you ain't wanting to be courting. Much less marrying the wench."

"I could not believe the prospect of spending time with her could be so bleak. I can't see how I'm going to go through with it."

"Don't have to, man. You know you don't have to."

"Good God, man—yes, I do. I've as good as asked the girl already. She's expecting it, and I'm expected to ask her. Beyond that, I've promised Mother."

"Give it up then, and stop complaining. Everyone knows that you're both hard-hearted. You and Lady Adelaide? Should be a perfect match."

"I know I'm hard-hearted, damne! Never cared for anyone in my whole life—save for my mother. Never felt the slightest desire for any woman—till the seventh of April, that is."

"What happened then?"

"Didn't I mention it? I suppose I didn't. I came home from the club, rather the worse for wine, and when I first saw her, I thought she wasn't even real."

" 'She'? What 'she'?"

"I'm getting to that. Thing is, I'd never seen a girl like that—fantastic! You know I've never been much in the petticoat line, and I've certainly never been drawn in by a woman's physical charms."

"That's the understatement of the era. You even paying enough attention to a woman to *notice* her physical charms? That's already a great shift away from the normal way of things."

"Don't like women. Don't like the whole sex. Never have."

"I know, I know. So?"

"So I saw this girl, standing on a streetcorner."

"Oh, really? How much was she?"

"Don't talk like that. She wasn't a light-skirt. She was just standing there, waiting in the fog and the lamplight. It's just—it was just that the very moment I saw her, something tremendous changed in me. I wanted her as I had never wanted a woman before."

"That's not saying much, is it?" said Lionel dryly.

"Do stop it, Lionel, and let me make myself perfectly clear. You know how much I wanted that pair of bays I saw in December?"

"Oh, rather! You spoke about them for months and months. Thought I'd never hear an end to it. Completely obsessed with them. I felt sorry for you."

"Well, Lionel, here's the ticket: I wanted that girl *more* than I wanted those bays."

"Did you, now?" said his friend, amazed.

"Beyond that: I wanted her more than I wanted to beat Tom Lundell at a sparring match."

"I say!" said Lionel, putting his glass down on the table with a smart crack.

"I didn't even know her. I didn't know who she was, or what she was, but in that instant—I was overcome with a desire that was, well, it was physical. I wanted to be—to be part of her and I wanted for her to be part of me."

"Let's not go into the sordid details, shall we? But I say this, Sarratt—you now have my full attention. I'm impressed. Tell me who was she? A young lady of quality, who had undergone some accident that left her momentarily stranded on the street until her chaperone returned with another conveyance?"

"No," said the duke glumly.

"Someone's poor relation, poor but well-born, one hopes?"

"No," said the duke with equal discontent.

"I assume now, that we're speaking of a diamond of the first water?"

"Very much so, but that isn't the point. In my lifetime, I have been introduced to scores of beautiful women, but none of them had the physical effect upon me that this one did. Once I met her, I began to dream of her. Once I saw her again, I couldn't put her out of my mind, even during the day. She'd be in Diana's room, and I'd find myself inventing excuses to go there; if she was with my mother, I'd find a reason to interrupt. If she were walking in the park, I'd try and go there, just to see her again. I'd see her in the hallway, dusting a mirror, and—"

"Beg pardon? Did you say 'dusting a mirror in the hallway,' Sarratt?"

"Yes," he said unhappily. "I'm afraid I did."

"Tell me, then, for I'm afraid I haven't got the run of it quite right. What, precisely, was this girl doing, in your house, in the hallway, dusting a mirror?"

Ready to reveal the worst at last, the duke whispered, "Because she's—she's our housemaid."

"Good God, man!" cried Lionel, slamming his fist down on the table in delight, and dissolving into raucous whoops of laughter. "Good God!

"But you can't *do* that, man! Not someone from your own household! Think of the servants!"

"I know, I know, I know. But don't you understand—I couldn't help it! I've never felt that way before, and I've not felt that way again, save for when I see her. Every time I see the chit, it's even worse!"

"This won't do. You're in a bad way, my dear Sarratt, and the results could be more untoward than you think. Be candid: are you telling me that you can't live without this chit?"

"I suppose I can't. I certainly don't wish to live without her."

Lionel gave his friend a clap on the back.

"Famous! Famous! The thing is, you've got to get her out of your house, and take her on as your mistress."

"Oh?" said the duke suspiciously.

"What else *can* you do with her, after all? Don't worry—it's a fine thing that has happened to you after all these years as a die-hard misogynist! Go ahead—let a little passion into your life, why don't you? Enjoy the solace that the warm arms of a woman can provide! Give yourself some consolation for having to marry that wretched Lady Adelaide."

"Well, I'd not considered that—it's a fascinating possibility. I've never had an official mistress, really. Not one that I really liked, at any rate. I always had a profound desire *not* to behave as my own father did, with a whole set of expensive ladybirds to the front, sides, and back of him."

"Don't be fustian! Don't talk like a Puritan! Take advantage of what Fate has brought you!"

"Are you sure?"

"Of course I am! Offer that girl *carte blanche*, man—she won't refuse you!"

"Very well, then. Very well."

Chapter 12

A few days after the duke's talk with the Hon. Lionel, it happened that Lady Mary Hamilton was set by the head housekeeper to the onerous chore of dusting each one of the books in his grace's personal library. This situation was, in Mary's view, a definite step upwards, as she didn't mind it as did many of the others, since she enjoyed being able to spend some time in quiet and solitude, for a change.

Lady Mary had already made good progress through the stacks of leather-bound books, and was examining one in particular which had caught her attention, when his grace himself chanced to enter the library. When he came in, the duke saw his exquisite maid-servant, not dusting, as she should have been, judging from her feather duster, but standing by the bookcase, deep in perusal of a book.

He walked over behind her, unseen, and took the book from her hands, causing her to jump.

"Oh! Your grace!"

"Shakespeare?" he asked, looking over the chosen book with interest.

"Yes, your grace," she nodded, blushed, and curtseyed. "I'm sorry, your grace. I know I was only supposed to clean it, not read it. I beg your pardon."

"You read this?"

"Yes, your grace. Well, I was only looking over *The Merchant of Venice,* not reading it all the way through. I hadn't the time. I was just browsing. I didn't mean to slack off. I had once learned by heart Portia's speech, but I had begun to forget some of it."

"I am intrigued."

"I like to recite things while I work—it makes cleaning much less tedious. I'm very sorry. I won't do it again."

"You are quite welcome to read in my library, in your odd moments, if you wish."

"Thank you, sir. You are very kind." Lady Mary was very conscious of how close the duke was standing to her. When Gervase had come this close to her, she had fled from him; the last thing Lady Mary wanted to do was to go away from the duke.

"Best not to be observed by the other servants, however. It might cause talk."

"Yes, of course, your grace."

"Now, what is your name again?"

"It is Mary, sir."

"Mary. Mary," he said, as if testing out the very sound of it.

Her very nearness was driving him to distraction; he was so close to her that he could smell the spicy scent of her hair. He wanted to be able to touch her, to crush her curls in his fingers whenever he wished, to bring her lips up to his if he felt the desire, to have her in his complete possession.

The duke decided at that moment that he could not,

he would not live without her, that he would indeed make his offer to her. It only remained to be seen precisely how he would make first mention of his proposal, which he decided to do in an indirect way.

"Who taught you to read, Mary?" he began. "I believe I asked you before, but I beg you will forgive me, I've forgotten what you said."

"My father taught me to read. He's dead now," she said, as if by way of explanation. "He loved books. He loved literature."

"Ah, yes. Now I recall. The unfortunate deacon with the extremely large family."

"Yes, your grace."

"Well, Mary, it seems a shame that you could not find more suitable outlets for your talents than going into service."

Lady Mary looked at her feet and blushed. Whatever did the man mean?

"I beg your pardon? Outlets more suitable to my talents?"

His grace stammered, something that he never did, normally, answering, "I—I only meant to suggest your accepting some other sort of . . . some sort of . . . other arrangement."

"Arrangement? I do not perfectly understand. Are you referring to a position as a companion, or as a governess, perhaps? I'm afraid I couldn't do that, sir. I just couldn't," she said, filled with conflicting emotions. She could hardly explain that a more visible position as companion or governess would have put her in jeopardy; for then she might be singled out and talked of among London society, and then Sir Barton Ayleston might trace her, come after her, and take her away.

A position as a governess or paid companion, however, was not what the duke had in mind.

"That is not quite what I meant, Mary. I meant that, perhaps, if you were so inclined, if you were willing, there might be some other—well, *arrangements* made that could be made more suitable to your liking."

The duke cast his eyes over the girl, and once again was aware of an intemperate beating of his heart. This was going to be far more difficult and awkward than his friend Fitzmartin had led him to believe.

"I am confused, your grace. You keep speaking about 'arrangements.' What arrangements do you mean?"

"Well, financial arrangements, for one thing. I am suggesting that perhaps someone could be found who would serve as—who might act—a person who would offer himself—what I mean is, one might find oneself a person who would vow to assume financial responsibility," he said, wishing he found the subject easier to speak of.

"Whyever would someone do that, sir?" she said, wide-eyed.

His grace was becoming increasingly frustrated, and swore under his breath.

Mary, beautiful Mary, was being incredibly, unbelievably obtuse. How could she be so naive? Couldn't she understand where this conversation was going? Did he have to put it down in writing?

He took a deep breath, tried to be patient, and tried again.

"Mary, I refer to someone who would offer you protection."

"Who?"

The duke took her small hand in his, and felt her hand begin to tremble.

"Myself, Mary."

To Mary, it was as if she had suddenly entered into the world of a dream. She could not believe he had taken her hand. What was happening? Her universe had undergone a sudden, mystical transformation.

She looked up at him with eyes filled with admiration and wonder.

"Sir, let me understand what you have said: can it be true, that you are offering me your protection?"

"Yes, Mary. I hope more than anything that you will consent to accept it. I will always be fair with you, and will always treat you with the respect and affection due to you."

Suddenly Mary became suffused with happiness. "Affection? Oh, your grace, I never dreamed—I am overwhelmed, and overjoyed. I don't see how this could have happened. I am so very much surprised, but—"

"But what?"

Lady Mary favored the duke with a blushing smile so lovely that he longed to sweep her into an embrace then and there.

"But I am also very happy, very deeply happy."

"That pleases me very much," said the duke, kissing her on her forehead, and taking her hand in his, pressing it meaningfully. "Mary. It is so good to be able to say your name at last: *Mary.*"

"I know it is so awkward to ask you this, but what is your Christian name?"

"Charles," said the duke tenderly. "You may call me Charles."

"It is so very hard to believe, Charles. You are really offering me the protection of your name?" said Mary, looking up at him, tears in her eyes, tears of happiness, love, and trust.

"My name?" said the duke, suddenly confused.

"Yes. Yes, of course. You are offering to marry me, sir, are you not?"

"I was offering *to keep you under my protection,*" said

his grace firmly, speaking in a clipped, formal tone meant to disabuse the silly chit of any more such awkward, irritating notions.

"What is that?" she asked. "What does that mean, precisely?"

"I was offering you *carte blanche,*" he said.

" 'White card'? Pray tell me, what is that?"

"Where were you brought up, child?" said his grace with asperity.

"I was brought up in Cumberland, though I don't see what that has to do with anything."

"Come, come, child: don't pretend. Everyone in London knows what *carte blanche* means!"

"Perhaps everyone in London knows what that phrase means, but I assure you, I do not!" she shot back, before she knew it. "Other than rendering those two words directly from the French, I have not the least idea what you are trying to say to me! I wish you will just tell me in plain words!"

"I am asking you to become my mistress!" he thundered, terribly angry now. "Will you do so?"

She had slapped him full across the face before she knew what she was doing, saying, "How dare you!"

Once aware of what she had done, she gasped.

His grace glowered, his hand gone to his cheek where she had slapped him, and it seemed for a moment that he might strike her back, but he merely stood there, speechless, livid.

Just then, the door flew open, and his friend Lord Weymouth bounded into the library and settled himself lazily into a chair. He tossed his curly beaver on the writing desk, a hat which his lordship had apparently neglected to hand over to the porter on arrival.

"Sarratt! Sorry for comin' in unannounced, old man, but the thing is—"

The earl stopped for just a moment, for he noticed that his old friend the duke was flushing bright red.

"Sarratt? Anything wrong?"

Weymouth looked hard at the duke, and then noticed the other person in the room. It took him not very long at all to notice that she was a female, a domestic, and an intensely lovely one at that.

Both their faces were bright red.

Lord Weymouth looked from one of them to the other, repeated that action, and then backed up apologetically, as if to leave.

"Sorry, old man. Take my leave now, shall I? See you later at the club, shall I? Have some things on which I'd like your opinion, when it's more convenient. Didn't mean to interrupt a private conversation."

The duke, cut to the quick, still furious, cut him off.

"What nonsense you speak, Weymouth. There is nothing here to interrupt. The girl was just going. She dropped a book, and I picked it up for her."

"Did you?" asked Lord Weymouth, uncommonly interested in this event.

"Yes. That will be all. Please leave us."

"Yes, your grace," snapped Lady Mary, as she curtseyed, and backed herself out of the room as fast as she could.

She wanted desperately to find a place so she could burst into tears in peace! How could the man insult her so? How could he have asked her to be his doxy, his ladybird, his Cyprian? How could she ever bear to look him in the face again, without wanting to slap him, again, and again, and again? She had never been so angry with anyone. She would have killed him in an instant, given the chance.

* * *

Even after Lady Mary had gone, and closed the door behind her, a dazzled Lord Weymouth continued to stare in her direction.

"Lovely creature, Sarratt. Magnificent. Works for you, does she?"

"Obviously so," said the duke, sarcastically, still livid. "For the nonce."

"Didn't mean to interrupt, old man. Said so before. None of my business, was it? Could have left at any time."

"There was nothing to interrupt, Weymouth! I already said that to you. Don't speak nonsense."

"But—there was that expression on your face, Sarratt," said the Earl of Weymouth, almost shyly. "Toward the girl. Were you perhaps unaware of it?"

"What expression?" cried the duke in shocked tones.

"Well, old man, how shall I put it? I've never seen the like upon your face in all my life, and I've known you since you were in leading-strings. It was a most singular thing. Your expression was almost—passionate."

"Passionate? I? Impossible!" asked the duke, now in a white fury. "You know perfectly well I'm not in the petticoat line. That was Father's predilection, it was never mine. It's pure nonsense. It's fustian. I'm not that kind of man; all my life I never have been, and everyone in London town knows it. I'm no romantic; I don't even *like* women! I never heard of such rubbish, and I wish you would stop."

"Charles, methinks thou dost protest too much. You looked at that girl with eyes brightened by profound pas-

sion. You looked as though you two had had a lovers'
quarrel."

"Rubbish! Weymouth, for all the love I bear you, you
shall turn the subject at once, do you hear? I command
you."

"If you say so, then certainly not. There was most
certainly *not* a look of utter admiration on your—"

"Weymouth!" he raged.

"Ease up, old man. Not the end of the world, is it?
No, but the thing is—that girl of yours—"

"She's *not* a girl of mine."

"Meaning that one that works for you, that pretty thing
I saw you talkin' to—I mean, dash it all, Sarratt, that
chit's a diamond of the first water. Which I now know
you're aware of, at least judging from your current
demeanor. The thing is, what's she doing working in your
household as a maid?"

"Whatever do you mean, Weymouth? She's employed
here. New girl. Housemaid. Dusts things."

"For one thing, it ain't proper. No one else in town
has maids like *that*, do they? Faces like hers don't belong
downstairs, no indeed they don't. Your Lady Adelaide
will tell you that, if you don't know it already, and so
would her grace, if she weren't so short-sighted as she
is. Probably her grace hasn't noticed what's come into
her household yet. Can't imagine what Buckley was
thinkin' of when he hired her—"

"Do stop."

"No, Sarratt, this is a serious thing, she don't belong
here—can't you see that? She'll cause all sorts of problems."

"*That* I can well believe," said the duke under his
breath.

"You must admit, Sarratt, the girl's a real wonder. That
face of hers should be her fortune, and the girl ought by

all rights to be down on Drury Lane, where she can take advantage of it, and make her mark in this world. Why, just the other day I met a chit who'd captivated Errol Gregson, and was fair on her way to ruining him, begging him for this little bauble and that one, but, as far as looks are concerned, that chit can't hold a candle to this one.''

''You and your incessant tales of the *demi-monde*— you'll never talk of anyone except your ladybirds. You should give them up, find a lady of quality, and settle down.''

''There's the pot calling the kettle black, Sarratt.'' Lord Weymouth's eyes narrowed. ''Why are you so obsessed with this girl?''

''I'm not obsessed with her! How should I be? I'm merely irritated when the subject is brought up, highly irritated.''

''Why does mention of her irritate you? You wanted the girl to yourself, is that what it's about? Did I interrupt you in the middle of making love to her? Perhaps you had made up your mind to offer the girl *carte blanche?''*

''No!'' said the duke mendaciously. ''I deny that. I don't do such things. I never have, and never will.''

''Don't be that way about it; you're a grown man, after all. Nothing wrong with having a ladybird.''

''I'm not a child, dammit! I know there's nothing wrong with keeping a woman!''

''Then what's got into you?''

''I'm angry because I *asked* her, and she *refused* me!'' thundered the duke.

''No! That's not possible!''

''It is possible! Furthermore, the girl slapped me full across my face! Expected me to marry her!''

''Well, that's impertinent of her, ain't it? Might even be termed insolent. Not the thing, in any case. Marrying the Duke of Sarratt? Bit above her touch.''

"Indeed so. I am happy to have escaped her toils, I can tell you. I am happy to have had her mercenary character revealed to me in such utter clarity. She almost made me feel guilty for having only offered to take her under my protection, but now I see her strategy for what it was, to use my passion to enslave me, and make me do her bidding.

"Marry her? What arrogance! What total, utter arrogance! The Duke of Sarratt, to join himself and his lineage to a *housemaid*? It's laughable!

"I'll tell you plainly, Weymouth, this incident has made me understand well what my proper direction must be. I am in control of my baser impulses, and shall give that girl no further thought than a snap of my fingers.

"I shall do my duty to my name, and I shall marry directly."

"Will you?" asked his friend, surprised. "Are you being serious now?"

The duke replied, "Certainly. If all this was the result of passion, I have had enough of 'passion.' But see here, Weymouth, I need a favor from you, for I must leave town at once. Would you escort Lady Adelaide to Ratcliffe's levee tomorrow night?"

"Let me have that maid of yours, if you're done with her, and I'll do anything that you wish."

"Weymouth!"

"Just joking, man. Where's your sense of humor? The chit seems to have robbed you of heart and humor both."

"*Will* you escort Lady Adelaide?"

"Tomorrow? Don't mind if I do. Like to see old Ratcliffe; he owes me some on account of that roan mare he backed, silly man. Happy to oblige you. Don't see why you're leavin' town if you've decided finally to give Adelaide the nod. What's the hurry?"

"I need time to think. This trip will allow me time to

make some decisions about the estate, and give me time to clear my head about my future.''

''You and Lady Adelaide really won't suit, you know. Knew it all along. Said so. You should think about it. Plenty of other fish in the sea. You could do better.''

''It's no matter. I don't care a fig if we suit or not, I'll marry the girl all the same. It's the right thing to do to uphold the honor of my family, joining our old and noble name with that of an equally ancient lineage. Care to make a wager on it?''

''Don't mind if I do. A thousand pounds, say?''

''Done. That I'll make Lady Adelaide Henchart my bride before the month's out!''

''Very well, Sarratt. It's your funeral.''

4 BESTSELLING HISTORICAL ROMANCES BY YOUR FAVORITE AUTHORS CAN BE YOURS, FREE!

Kensington Choice, our newest book club now brings you historical romances by your favorite bestselling authors including Janelle Taylo Shannon Drake, Rosanne Bittner, Jo Beverley, and Georgina Gentry, just to name a few! Each book is filled with passion, adventure and th excitement of bygone times!

To introduce you to this great new club which is part of Zebra Home Subscription Service, we'd like to send you your first 4 bestselling historical romances, absolutely free! And once you get these 4 free books to savor at home, we'll rush you the next 4 brand-new books a the lowest prices available, as soon as they are published.

The way the club works is that after your initial FREE shipment, yo will get our 4 newest bestselling historical romances delivered to you

doorstep each month at the preferred subscriber's rate o only $4.20 per book, a savings of up to $7.16 p month (since these titles sell in bookstores for $4.99 $5.99)! All books are sent on a 10-day free examination basis and ther is no minimum number of books to buy. (A postage and handling charge $1.50 is added to each shipment.) Plus as a regular subscriber, you'll receive our FREE monthly newsletter, *Zebra/Pinnacle Romance News*, which features author profiles, contests, subscriber benefits, book previews and mor

So start today by returning the FREE BOOK CERTIFICATE provided. We'll send you 4 FREE BOOKS with no further obligation: A FREE gift offering you hours of reading pleasure with no obligation...how can you lose?

We have 4 FREE BOOKS for you
as your introduction to
KENSINGTON CHOICE!
To get your FREE BOOKS, worth
up to $23.96, mail the card below.

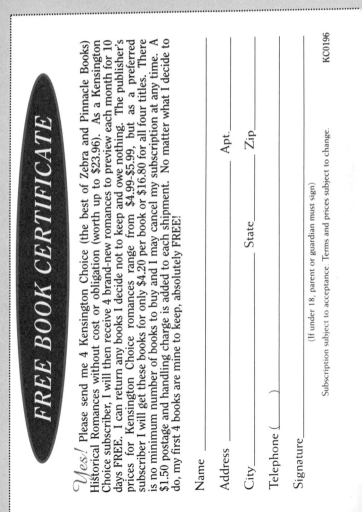

FREE BOOK CERTIFICATE

Yes! Please send me 4 Kensington Choice (the best of Zebra and Pinnacle Books) Historical Romances without cost or obligation (worth up to $23.96). As a Kensington Choice subscriber, I will then receive 4 brand-new romances to preview each month for 10 days FREE. I can return any books I decide not to keep and owe nothing. The publisher's prices for Kensington Choice romances range from $4.99-$5.99, but as a preferred subscriber I will get these books for only $4.20 per book or $16.80 for all four titles. There is no minimum number of books to buy and I may cancel my subscription at any time. A $1.50 postage and handling charge is added to each shipment. No matter what I decide to do, my first 4 books are mine to keep, absolutely FREE!

KC0196

Name _____

Address _____ Apt._____

City _____ State_____ Zip_____

Telephone ( ) _____

Signature _____

(If under 18, parent or guardian must sign)

Subscription subject to acceptance. Terms and prices subject to change.

AFFIX
STAMP
HERE

KENSINGTON CHOICE
Zebra Home Subscription Service, Inc.
120 Brighton Road
P.O.Box 5214
Clifton, NJ 07015-5214

Chapter 13

Sam Boswell, the duke's valet, had never before seen his grace in such a blind rage, and it lasted throughout dinner, throughout the next, and full into the next morning. His rage took the form of finding fault with everything.

Suddenly, his grace's port wine was too young; the brandy too bitter; the claret unspeakably bad. His grace sent back his pheasant, untouched. His conversation at dinner had been monosyllabic at best; his dismayed mother and his ward were perfectly happy to learn of his plans to leave town, he had been such an unentertaining presence at the table.

In the morning, having packed his things for the trip to the country, it was quite the same. Boswell was informed that all the duke's cravats were ill-made, the cut of his coats was incorrect, the colors were wrong, the cloth was wrong, everything had been badly conceived and badly executed. His mirror-bright Hessians were found to have minute, marring scratches, despite the long hours dedicated to their polishing, done with Sam's own secret champagne-based formula.

The fact was, the duke was horribly angry with himself. His intellect had become shockingly, painfully aware that he had become emotionally entangled with one of his staff. He thought it nauseating. Of course, it would not do, not at all. Through such rash, unthinking, unsuitable behavior, he might well have demeaned the name of Wellesford.

How had it happened? After all these years of being perfectly impervious to female wiles, how had he succumbed at last? How had he succumbed to the charms of someone so unsuitable?

Was it the influenza? Familial insanity?

Surely, a fever could easily be held responsible for these intense physical sensations that seemed to be wreaking havoc with his intelligence. Intellectually, he realized he was acting in an unseemly manner; it was madness, sheer madness.

What if his mother or his ward had entered during that interview, rather than Lord Weymouth? What would they have thought of him, standing there with a red face, stammering like a schoolboy, trying to entice a lower servant into an immoral liaison? How had he become captivated by her? How could he escape?

Had the propensities he had always abhorred in his own father suddenly arisen in him? It was *that* possibility that was most grim.

He had made his decision: out of sight, out of mind. He would leave town, he would cure himself of this wretched attachment, and he would come back and do what he ought to have done long ago.

*   *   *

Mary had cried all that night, and into the next morning; she had not slept all night, but had taken her small hard pillow out into the hall and wept there, afraid that if Susan heard her she would box her ears again.

What did he think of her, to make an offer like that? In what low esteem did he hold her? It was horrible to contemplate. She knew, in some part of herself, that given what he had been told of her birth and circumstances, it was an unsurprising offer, but still, it left her pride deeply wounded.

When, from an upstairs window, Lady Mary saw the duke leave the house the next morning, driving himself out to Broadbrooke in his curricle, she was glad to see him go. She was still in no position to resign from her position and leave the house, as she wished to do, but she wanted desperately not to have to come face to face with the man—not ever again. It was too lowering.

Fate intervened on Mary's behalf once again, when Buckley called her down to his room again, and offered her a promotion to a new position: that of Miss Diana's personal maid. Would she care to take it on? he inquired.

She answered that she would very much like to do so. It was a change that helped abate her fury at the duke, and her humiliation at the offer he had made to her. Perhaps she would be better able to avoid contact with him once she was spending more time in Miss Diana's boudoir, where his grace never ventured.

Buckley let Mary know that it was chiefly the dowager who had been behind the offer of promotion. Mary was a bit surprised by this, but was enthusiastic about the change.

Her grace had been pleased and relieved when Buckley told her he had questioned Mary Simpson at length, and that any concerns the dowager might have as to her character should be laid to rest. Mr. Buckley had assured her grace that Mary betrayed no vulgar origins such as would disbar her from serving in the household, but that, on the contrary, her origins were determined to have been at the very least respectable.

Hearing this, the dowager had made it clear that, in such a case, she considered Mary unsuited to continue working as an under-housemaid, and that Buckley was to try to find a more appropriate position for her upstairs, or see if some more suitable employment could be found for her in another household. Her grace was someone who liked all persons to assume their proper positions in the social order

Buckley, who had taken a distinct liking to Mary for her simple unassuming ways and quiet dignity, was not anxious to lose her to another great house. He mentioned to her grace that since Miss Diana's governess had left service in order to marry some months before, Miss Diana had been left on her own, with neither companion nor personal maid to look after her interests. Perhaps, he had suggested gently, Mary Simpson might be elevated to this task, particularly since Miss Diana was now out, and since Farley, the duchess's own dresser, felt herself too old to look after a duchess and a girl trying to cut a dash in her first season.

The duchess had said that she thought it a splendid idea, and immediately sent for Diana. Diana concurred with enthusiasm, and Buckley rang for Mary, who immediately accepted her new position, doing so with grace and gratitude, saying that she hoped very much to do credit to her new mistress. Privately she hoped that she would be better able to avoid the duke and his unwanted advances as well.

*   *   *

Mary's promotion brought her very own pallet, laid down in a sort of closet next to Miss Diana Leigh's dressing room, off the bedchamber. The pallet was much softer than Mary's lumpy flock mattress in the attic had been, and of course it only had one occupant, herself. The tiny closet room seemed to Lady Mary to be a place of almost heavenly rest and perfect privacy. There was no bellicose, snoring Susan, and the bedcovers were almost sufficient to keep her warm.

The first night that she moved in, she took advantage of this privacy; she took out her mother's jewels from the black velvet bag again, and spread them out to look at them. Emeralds and sapphires, rubies and diamonds: it was remarkable what a source of solace they were. They reminded her of her real, and loving parents; they reminded her of the noble family from which she was, by good fortune, descended; they reminded her of a whole world to which she belonged and would one day rejoin— if she could remain safe from the machinations of her stepfather's family. Save for her lowering encounter with the duke, things seemed to be working out well.

On impulse Lady Mary took a thin golden satin riband and threaded it through the Hamilton ruby ring—the one with the crest that her father had always worn on the third finger of his right hand until the day of his death. After his death, his widow had threaded a black riband through it, and had worn it next to her heart until the day that she, too, left this world. Lady Mary Hamilton thought that if she, too, wore that ring constantly, it would be a way to draw from its dark ruby depths some solace and some strength, which she felt in need of.

She placed it over her neck, and tucked it in. Instantly it made her feel better.

Lady Mary thought the sudden improvement in her circumstances marvelous, a welcome example of the adage that even dark clouds may have silver linings. It would be much more pleasant to be upstairs darning Miss Diana's dresses than to be scurrying through the backstairs hallways, where Susan Bowker would pass her by and give her a box on her ears, just to be mean.

Lady Mary wanted to write to Fanny to tell her, but she had very little cash money left, and she was loath to part with what she had, lest she require it urgently. There was almost nothing extra with which to pay for a letter; there was nothing she had save the Hamilton jewels, still safe in their black velvet bag.

She tried not to think of her unhappy past, of the unhappiness attached to the duke, to Gervase and to Sir Barton. Rather, she tried to think of the future, her life at Sarratt House until her majority, and then of her happier life thereafter.

In the near future, life would be much easier, for, besides having been selected to ascend to the ranks of the Upper Ten, the tasks she would perform as a young lady's maid were to her liking. Instead of herself having to lay the fire in Miss Diana's bedroom, or pass the sheet-warmer between the covers in the evening, she would merely see to it that it had been done properly by one of the lower housemaids.

She would be responsible for waking Miss Diana, discussing with her the clothes she would wear, and laying them out for her. She would bring in to Miss Diana a ewer of hot water in which to wash, but now hers would not be the hands that had hauled the water in great brass cans up three flights of stairs.

She would then spend a good half an hour brushing Miss Diana's hair. It occurred to her that her dusky blonde hair might be brightened by applications of lemon juice, and drying the hair in the sun, if they could find any private place to do so. She would have to wrap Miss

Diana's face up, of course, to protect her complexion, but it was a good idea, the lemon. She would try it, with her mistress's permission.

She would help the young lady to put on the actual garments that had been chosen, checking them meticulously for rips or stains, making sure the fastenings were properly done. She would suggest a style of hair suitable to her lady's activities, and help to achieve that look.

After her mistress was ready for the day, and went downstairs, her personal maid would not even be required to make her bed, but would ring again for a housemaid. Mary would have to look after any personal items Miss Diana had tossed about the room: picking up ribands, putting away jewelry, matching gloves, cleaning her silver-backed combs and brushes and putting them in order.

The very hardest part of the job would be being responsible for the care of her wardrobe. She must be sure that Miss Diana's clothes were always clean, sweet-smelling, well-brushed, and free of stains, for, even though young ladies of quality were taught to be careful with their clothes, long garments did tend to gather mud at their hems, and gowns were always being exposed to dripping candlewax, even at the most exclusive social engagements, and that wax could be very tricky to remove.

Mary would be there to help curl Miss Diana's hair at night, and would spend time preparing restorative potions for her mistress's face—that at least would be easy enough, for her own mother and her lady's maid, Ann, had been geniuses in that area of feminine wisdom. She would act on Miss Diana's behalf, just as her own mother and maid had done for her when she had broken out in those awful red spots.

So it would be, her life as an abigail.

And after that, after she had safely reached twenty-one? She would sell some of the jewels, perhaps the garnet set, and she would buy herself an extremely nice walking dress, in white trimmed with pink, and with a matching parasol and slippers and white gloves.

She would ask for a morning off, and dress herself to the nines. She would leave from the servants' area door, of course, and everyone would be talking about her—especially Susan Bowker! She would only smile at their questions, say good-bye, and hire herself a hackney. She would have the hackney let her off at the offices of Thorpe and Middletown, and she would send in to them her name, Lady Mary Hamilton, sole heiress to the late Earl and Countess of Hamilton.

Her life would begin again there. They would cause a townhouse to be rented for her, they would arrange for the staff and the furnishings, and a carriage. She would engage an older companion so as to maintain the proprieties, and an abigail, of course. She would order a fabulous wardrobe to be made, and she would begin to live the life her parents had intended she should have.

Lady Mary Hamilton knew that it was vital that she maintain her deception, and remain safely hidden in the Duke of Sarratt's household, no matter that the very picture of him coming to her mind afforded her pain.

Her deception must continue until her birthday, even at the cost of her pride; her happiness, indeed her future life depended on it.

Chapter 14

It was unconscionably late that same night when, far away in the wilds of Cumberland, there came an insistent knocking on the door of the baronet's bedchamber. Sir Barton Ayleston wished, and not for the first time, that his relatives and retainers could develop more delicacy of behavior, but he knew this to be hopeless.

"Sir Barton!" cried the loud voice from the corridor, making its recipient wince. "Have you retired for the evening, or will you admit us now?"

Hearing this, Sir Barton Ayleston slapped the wench known as Sal Orden twice on her ample haunches, and sent her on her way through the dressingroom door that she generally used. He told her to be sure not to wake up his man as she passed, and that he would see her again tomorrow night.

He threw on a gaudy brocade dressing-gown, knotted it firmly, and looked in the glass to see if his hair was unkempt. It was not, but he took his silver-backed brush to it anyway, for he was a proud kind of person.

Sir Barton, a dark-haired man with a thin mustache had business to attend to that was so important it could no be postponed until morning. Hastily hiding some papers i his desk, he called out, "Enter!"

The door opened to admit two persons: his nephew Gervase, and a henchman, Duncan Baker.

"Well?" said the baronet.

"Sir, she's not gone to Scotland, we're sure of tha now," said Duncan Baker. Duncan was a pale, rotun person who, no matter how carefully he dressed, alway seemed as if he had just emerged from a cellar, or storage bin.

"Are we sure that she's not gone there?" replied S: Barton with a sneer. "Are we sure? It was her most likel destination."

No one replied for a moment. Gervase and Duncan stared at one another for a moment, unwilling to be th person venturing a reply. Finally Gervase took the bu by the horns.

"Yes, Uncle, we're sure" said Gervase, a youth wit a sharp nose, and green gimlet eyes which did not alway look in the same direction. He fiddled nervously with hi cravat as he admitted, "We asked everyone there was t ask if a Lady Mary Hamilton had been known to sta there, or travel through there, or if she made arrangement to take stages or reside with local families. We sper money very freely making inquiries; we left no ston unturned."

"Spending my blunt at it, or your blunt?"

"Well, that is, your blunt, Uncle, but you—"

"That is perhaps why you felt it necessary to spend so freely. And to spend it without result."

"But, Uncle, you said to find her, no matter what took."

"That, my boy, is precisely the point. You must fin

er, and you will find her. You spent my money freely, and yet you did *not* find her, did you?"

"No, Uncle, but at least, as a direct result of our labor in the search, we know now, with great precision, where not to look. This in itself is quite encouraging, is it not?"

Sir Barton tapped a long finger on the mantelpiece and gave the two men a look of long-suffering impatience.

"God protect me! Gervase, Gervase, whatever am I to do with you?"

"With me, sir?"

"Oh, never mind. It's hopeless."

"I don't follow you."

"Yes, exactly. See here, Gervase, I must confess at this point that I am overwhelmed by your perspicacity. Having spent God knows how much of my funds, you come here and, in the most self-satisfied of manners, inform me that I may be happy, for I know where we need *not* look. We need *not* look for Lady Mary in Gretna Green, is that it? Is that what you've come here to tell me?"

"Yes, sir!" said Gervase, pleased that he'd gotten his point across at last. "We do know that, sir, now, certainly."

"It's very good work we did," chimed in Baker. "We thought sure she'd gone there, didn't we?"

"My *dear* Baker, my most *esteemed* nephew Gervase, how very remiss of me! I seem to have failed to fully appreciate your handiwork. That you have spent heaven knows how many golden guineas of my fortune—"

"It's the Hamilton fortune, really, Uncle—"

"It is *my* money now, Gervase, and the rest of it will be *our* money soon enough, if you use your head and do as you're told. Have a care, Gervase! Learn to husband your resources more wisely! You have spent a goodly sum of family money and gone to a good deal of trouble, and have returned home to Danby to tell me proudly that

you have narrowed down the possibilities of Lady Mary
hiding place. The area of search is merely the entir
remaining area of the British Isles," he said with col
sarcasm. "Save for the town of Gretna Green in Scotlane
of course. Splendid work, gentlemen, splendid wor
indeed!"

It had taken all this time for Sir Barton to make hi
point, and finally he had done so. Baker and Gervas
braced for the inevitable storm to come.

It took no more than an instant to hit. Sir Barton Ayles
ton slammed his fist onto the sideboard, causing the cup
and plates to jump and rattle.

"Have you no more information than that, dolts? Wha
is my good money paying for? I don't even see why yo
thought that she would have gone on to Gretna in th
first instance."

"That's what you told us."

"Nothing of the sort. It was merely that she had escape
from us at the border, so very near to our destination, it
most annoying.

"Look here, Duncan—I must and will have informa
tion on this girl!"

"Then we must hire more men, sir."

"Do it! But you must find out what has become c
her! The time in which we can act against her is limitec
She must be back safely in our hands while she is sti
in her minority, and while I am still her legal guardiar
I must have her back, right away!"

"We will bring her back, Uncle."

"Yessir, Sir Barton. That we will."

"Your assurances are meaningless. How, I ask yo
under your very noses, did she escape from us in the fir
instance? Please explain it to me. I should like very muc
to understand how a weak inexperienced young girl, per
niless and completely unused to the ways of the worlc

is struck on the head, successfully abducted, taken senseless in our carriage and rushed toward the border, and left, still senseless, safely locked in an inn run by people most sympathetic to our cause—and yet somehow simply vanishes into thin air."

"It won't happen again, Uncle."

"Spare me your worthless words, and bring Lady Mary to me! A girl possessed of such extraordinary beauty—it should have been the easiest thing in the world to track her down. She should have been recaptured long ago. By now, she should have been Lady Mary Ayleston, Gervase, your lawfully wedded and bedded wife."

"Yes, Uncle."

Sir Barton sat down at a table and pulled out a map.

"Here, gentlemen: I will outline for you precisely how the thing should be done. I feel that I have done so before, but I had thought that even you could not be so scatterbrained about it. The thing is this: obtain a map of the vicinity. Following a circular pattern, hire in each and every town falling within that circle a single, well-paid informant."

"Well-paid, Uncle? Do I understand that now you are saying we are to spend money freely again on gaining information?"

"I don't know whose blood runs in those veins of yours, Gervase, for it certainly is not the same as that which runs through mine. Let me explain it once again. If you hire an informant, and overpay him for the job, he will wish to perform his services well for you in hopes you may hire him again, and once more overpay him. Hiring the informants in the area of the circle surrounding Danby Court means that each and every possible avenue of Lady Mary's escape will have been covered."

"Yes, Uncle."

"It is a question of logic, not magic. *Someone* will

have seen her. Someone *must* have seen her. Someone must remember her. Some ostler at an inn, some waitress at an eating-house, some delivery boy making his rounds, some farmboy bringing in his cart to a village will have seen that girl. And having seen her, would not forget her face, for as we know, Lady Mary's visage is quite remarkable. It will, in the end, be her downfall.

"You may show them this."

He took out of his pocket a small golden frame with a miniature portrait in it. The portrait was one that had been done years before of the Countess of Hamilton, but it was as like to Lady Mary as if she had sat for it herself.

"That's what was needed, Uncle. We'll find her easily now. Anyone who has seen her should be able to recognize her now."

"Precisely," said Sir Barton.

He motioned Duncan to pour him a drink, and he quaffed it greedily.

In a tone of characteristic self-congratulation, he said, "It was both wise and fortunate that I arranged to have her left in splendid isolation, far from the ton, for if I had not, her identity as Lady Mary Hamilton, the earl's sole heir, would have been impossible to conceal. Trying to arrange for you, Gervase, to marry with an heiress well-known to society would have been impossible; the whole plan would have come to nothing.

"But, Gervase, luckily for you I am a patient man, and have worked many long years to bring the fullness of the Hamilton fortunes within my purview. First the mother, then the child: it has taken me a good ten years to see it to its final settlement, but my plan has been masterful in all respects. Through your marriage to this girl, we shall cause the re-establishment of the Hamilton lineage through ennobling our own. You shall change your name, accordingly, to Hamilton. You yourself shall take control of all the Hamilton estates. Your own firstborn son shall become the first Earl of Hamilton of the Second Creation. Is it not wonderful?

"There remains only this one small error to correct: the girl must be found and brought back within our custody. And married. At once."

"But, Uncle—"

"Don't mewl at me, Gervase. Go out and bring her back here! Let's be done with it."

"Yes, Uncle."

Chapter 15

The absence of the Duke of Sarratt made matters more simple for several of its occupants. There were to be no complicated dinners, which pleased all the staff, giving them time to catch up on their various seasonal labors. The delivery by Thomas, the footman, of the duke's hastily written letter of apology to Lady Adelaide, explaining his abrupt decision to go to Broadbrooke, resulted in a complete cessation of Lady Adelaide's visits to the dowager, a circumstance which pleased the duke's ward completely. The Hon. Lionel Fitzmartin and Lord Weymouth as well ceased to call; this change saddened Diana Leigh, for she had always enjoyed the earl's company, even though he regarded her rather in the light of a little sister.

The morning after the duke left town for Broadbrooke, Lady Mary Hamilton was sent upstairs to work for the first time. In her mind, she had dedicated the day to making herself acquainted with the whole of Miss Diana's extensive wardrobe. She was guided in this task by Farley, the duchess's dresser, who had had charge of it until Mary was called to the task.

"I can tell you I'm pleased to have another pair of hands to do the work around here. Miss Diana should have had proper help of her own long ago, if you ask me. When that governess went, they shilly-shallied around for a ridiculous amount of time before they realized that the girl was old enough to need some help of her own.

"Miss Diana's just at that particularly awkward age—not so grown up that she won't climb a tree in a good muslin gown—and I won't hide from you that I'm good and tired of trying to get those dratted grass stains out—but not so young that she doesn't want to look well turned out when Lord Weymouth comes to call.

"Her grace of Sarratt is enough to look after. While I love Miss Diana dearly, I am getting too long in the tooth myself to deal with her sulks."

"Sulks?" said Lady Mary, wondering for just a moment whether this would be really a step up at all.

"Just you wait. She has a little temper, can Miss Diana; it only takes a word from Lady Adelaide to put her out of mood. It used to take me the whole rest of the day to try and wheedle her out of it. Make sure you leave plenty of time for wheedling the girl—it's part of the job."

"I see," said Lady Mary, rather alarmed.

"We can rearrange these gowns later, and I'll show you where I've put the mending materials, and the pins and tapes and the clothes brushes. Why don't you go on in and draw the drapes, and ask Miss if she's ready for her chocolate?"

Mary scratched on the door, went in, and curtseyed. Miss Diana Leigh, the duke's ward, was still curled around her pillow.

"Good morning, Miss," said Mary, opening the drapes so the delicate morning light spilled into the bedroom.

Far below, one could hear the sounds of an awakening city; Lady Mary still hadn't gotten used to how very noisy London was.

"Good morning. Oh! It's not Farley, is it? It's you!"

"Yes, Miss."

"What's your name, again? Wasn't it Mary?"

"Yes, Miss."

"I'm so glad. I had asked if you would like to come to work for me. I hope that's all right with you. Is it?"

"Very much so, Miss."

She popped her feet out of the bedcovers and stretched like a cat. Then she took off her lacy nightcap and flung it across the room, aiming for a chair, but watching it land on the floor. Lady Mary walked over to it, picked it up, brushed it off, folded it, and put it away in Miss Diana's dresser, and then she did the same for Miss Diana's stockings and scarf and hair-combs.

"I hope you didn't think it unhandsome of me when I did not take your hand the other day," said her new mistress. "I feel I behaved shabbily toward you. I didn't mean to do so; I was just stunned for a moment. Will you forgive me?"

"No, no; it was my mistake, Miss. I'm very sorry. I don't know what I could have been thinking. So embarrassing for me."

"No matter at all. According to Nana, you have talked with Buckley, I take it? And everything has been straightened out?"

"Yes, Miss."

"Well, I'm very glad of it. It will be nice to have someone around me nearer my own age."

"Shall I bring up your chocolate?"

Lady Mary pulled the bell twice, which was the signal for Cook to dole out the hot chocolate, and give the tray to an upper housemaid to deliver upstairs. She backed out of Miss Diana's room, and went to wait at the top of the servants' staircase.

In but a few minutes, who should appear with the tray but Susan Bowker.

"Here you go, Yer Highness. You must be pleased to be livin' upstairs now, rubbin' shoulders with the quality, aren't you? Well, I hopes you don't dump this tray an' make a mess like you did the *last* one."

"Don't talk to me like that, Susan."

"Why not? What's different now? Think you're too good for the rest of us now, now that yer sinkin' the beer like all them other servants who acts as if they're not servants but masters—*our* masters, lording it over the rest of us? Think yer a better person, now that yer havin' yer wine and talkin' fancy talk, way up there in heaven, up in Pug's Parlor? Well, you just wait and see," she said mysteriously. "Better watch yer step, missy. Don't you forget it: even the mighty can fall."

Within just a few days, after minor mutual adjustments, Lady Mary Hamilton and the Honorable Diana Leigh were soon on the very best of terms. Diana was very pleased to have someone around to talk to who was not acting toward her in the role of guardian, like Uncle Charles or the dowager—someone younger and of her own sex, and a person who was much more *au courant* with styles of hair and of dress than Farley. Diana liked Mary's gentle manner, her sharp sense of humor, and the careful attention she paid to her. She also was deeply appreciative of Mary's throwing herself into her working of looking after her new mistress, and working to present Diana in the most flattering possible light.

Following the particular advice the Countess of Hamilton had given her, Mary advised her new charge of what dishes she should eat, and what foods to avoid, in order to maintain good health and a good figure. Turbot with lobster sauce or any kind of game bird, she said, was perfectly acceptable; venison, saddle of mutton, and all the heavier viands were best avoided, wherever possible. However, it was important not to engage in excessive dietary rigors, such as following, like that scandalous Byron, a harsh diet of biscuits and water.

The two girls pored over issues of the magazines showing the latest modes, with particular attention toward the color fashion plates in *The Lady's Magazine,* and *La Belle Assemblee.* At Diana's express behest, with the active connivance of the dowager duchess, the three women began in earnest to enhance Miss Diana Leigh's wardrobe. Deprived of Lady Adelaide's baneful influence, Diana began to take real interest in shopping on Bond Street, and gave new attention to the serious business of appearing always at her best.

Over the course of that first week, the three women reviewed every gown Diana owned: they made a list of them; they divided them into categories and sub-categories; they criticized their shortcomings in terms of style, color, cut and fabric. They gave away (mainly to Mary) those gowns that were for some reason found unsuitable, ridding the wardrobe of those colors such as pea-green and pomona green that Diana must never wear, and purchasing fabrics in those colors such as clarence blue and carmine that most became her.

The fact was, Mary was much more at ease working at the top of the house. She had begun to sleep longer, and more deeply, in the comparative privacy of the closet next to Miss Diana's dressingroom. Not having to do so much heavy carrying and cleaning, Mary felt much more relaxed and at ease, and indeed, enjoyed the lively company of her new mistress. Upstairs, of course, she was much more in her own natural element.

Lady Mary had a very good sense of style, one instilled

in her by her own mother, and she shared these opinions with Diana very generously. She could tell where a seam should be, and where it had no business to be; she knew how to speak to a seamstress in language that the seamstress appreciated, understood, and respected.

Her spirits elevated, Mary began virtually to throw herself into her work. Her skills as a needlewoman, developed over many housebound Cumberland winters, were obvious and much-needed; she could redo a seam in a flash; she could invisibly mend even the most rampant tear in a lace flounce.

It soon turned out that Mary had a natural flair for dressing hair: her nimble fingers could twist papers quickly and firmly, they could coax curls out of thin air, and she knew just how to arrange a fall of curls so as to have the effect seem perfectly natural.

Lady Mary proved to be a positive genius at concocting facial potions: out of a variety of sweet smelling (for the most part) components, she brewed creams and balms. She invented a lotion of lemon and crushed strawberries particularly designed to banish Diana's freckles, and a pink, chamomile-based concoction to repair the occasional blemish.

As part of her beauty campaign, she persuaded her mistress to constantly wear gloves, both outside and inside, something Diana had previously, out of an excess of adolescent willfulness and a dislike of taking Lady Adelaide's orders, been loath to do. Mary was able to persuade Diana to forgo wearing hats with shallow pokes, which exposed her sensitive skin to the sun, and begin a new dedication to high pokes and parasols. Soon, Diana never went out without protection, and soon enough, the freckles she had been so ashamed of began to fade. Miss Diana thought her new maid a positive miracle, and as her once-brown complexion began to improve, so did her temper.

The dowager quickly grew to appreciate both Mary's talents and her stability of character. Her grace regarded Mary's influence on Diana Leigh with distinct approbation. She herself grew to depend upon Mary, who was always willing to run errands for her if Farley were otherwise occupied, or to find lost objects, or to read to her at length. She performed offices nearer to those of companion than those of merely a maid and dresser; the rest of the household, both above and belowstairs were also very appreciative of her, with the exception of Susan Bowker, who still held her in particular dislike.

Lady Mary Hamilton had finally proven herself, and in so doing, she earned an invaluable position in the household; she was able to dash off a note to Fanny Simpson to the effect that, with her most recent rise in station, she had no doubts of being able to last in service incognita till her birthday. Her situation, so rocky at the beginning, was taking a turn for the better.

At the end of seven days of intensive labor, a full report on the state of Diana's wardrobe was presented to the dowager, who found herself much in agreement with what they had decided.

Her grace said that she would bring the topic to the duke's attention upon his expected return tomorrow from Broadbrooke, for the financial outlay necessary for purchasing all these necessary items would be substantial. The cost of an evening ballgown alone, made of sheer satin, trimmed with seed-pearls, lace, and satin rosebuds, might be several hundred pounds—if not more.

Chapter 16

Blue sky! Never before had it seemed so magnificent, such a thing of splendor and freedom! How good it seemed to Lady Mary to see the sky again, after so many weeks spent in lightless corridors and ill-lit chambers swathed in draperies, even if it was the sky only as viewed through the chimneys of brick buildings—a London blue sky, grayed by coal smoke.

Mary's freedom was bought at the price of her pride, since it meant she had gone out of the house on errands accompanying her mistress, walking a respectful pace behind her, carrying bandboxes or whatever packages she had accumulated. Her menial circumstances were of no great consequence; it was all well worth it to Lady Mary Hamilton. It was such a happy thing to be out and about amongst the wider world once again.

And of course, it was London! Bustling, clamoring, clattering universe—it was such great fun for a girl brought up, for the most part, in deepest Cumberland. To be taken up in the duke's elegant and shining crest-

emblazoned coach with Miss Diana and driven to Bond
Street to shop—it was like a fairytale. At the very least
going out to shop with her was an adventure filled with
pleasures; being able to help her new mistress select from
so many exquisite fabrics and colors and patterns was
like being a small child let loose in a candy-land.

Fashions were becoming ever more elaborate, and with
the advent of her first season, Diana was being called
upon to attend ever more gatherings which required ever
more garments: dinner dresses, evening dresses, morning
dresses, carriage dresses. She needed dresses for walking,
riding, and attending the opera and the theater. She needed
matching spencers and shawls and pelisses. And of course
she needed the full round of hats to go with every outfit,
and gloves, and slippers.

The two women fussed over buying each and every
riband and frill and furbelow—the two young girls, not so
far apart in age, were having the greatest time imaginable,
particularly since the duke had been so generous as to
allow his ward free rein in spending.

Spend they did—for example, Diana bought a white
morning dress with ten blue satin ribands circling the hem
at one-inch intervals. The bodice and cuffs were similarly
adorned with rows of ribands, and there was a fetching
half-moon collar. Diana was deeply pleased, for she
thought she looked quite the thing in it.

They packed all their purchases into the duke's town
coach, and were about to order the coachman to take them
home, when they heard a familiar voice.

"Diana!" said Lady Adelaide Henchart. "How very
good to see you! I had hoped I might run into you some
time. How have you been?"

"Very well, thank you," she replied unenthusiastically.

"Shopping again, are you?"

"Yes."

"You're *so* fortunate you don't have to worry about buying gowns that are too dear. If I were an heiress, I'm sure I'd just fritter away whatever I had on a million trifles, which is, I suppose, just what you've been doing, you naughty girl! Now I hope you haven't been buying those lemon-yellow muslins, again, as I particularly told you you should not. The color, though you prefer it, certainly makes your sallowness appear much worse. I'm surprised you're not out shopping with an older, more experienced lady, such as the dowager or myself, to steer you away from unsuitable purchases. Going out only with a maid when one is young and foolish is really very dangerous."

At this point Lady Adelaide deigned to look behind Diana at her abigail.

"Oh!" she said, in most disapproving tones. "You have a *housemaid* acting as your *abigail?* That won't do, you know, Diana. It really will not do. One really must have a French maid, you know. I do, of course. Whyever did the dowager countenance such an odd arrangement? Does her grace know about it?"

"She knows about it, and approves."

"Well! I'm sure I don't know what to say! Diana, just between you and me: take my counsel—don't let that *creature* come around with you. It's very unsuitable, and besides, you can't hold a candle to her, so it does *you* no good at all, does it? Men will follow you around merely so they can get a glimpse of your maid."

"Thank you for your sage advice, Lady Adelaide," snapped Diana Leigh.

"You really *must* learn to hold that temper of yours in check, Diana. It is very unbecoming in a young lady of quality. Oh, and here we have Lord Weymouth! What a happy coincidence!"

"How do you do, ladies?"

"We are very well, thank you," said Lady Adelaide. "How very auspicious that we all have met here. I must know at once if you have heard of the duke's plans. When will he return from Broadbrooke?"

"I had not thought he would remain very much above a week."

Lady Adelaide clapped her hands.

"Marvelous! He will be back in time for Lord Marshall's ball! Shall you be going, Lord Weymouth?"

"I am afraid not. I have a musical engagement."

"Of what kind?" asked Diana.

"I had forgotten that you are a great fan of music, Miss Leigh. You may be interested in what I have in mind. I have obtained a special music-master from Austria, and he will be playing for me on that evening, and instructing me in some particularly complex pieces I wish to learn how to play myself."

"Fascinating! How lucky you are! I wish I could do something of that sort!"

"Diana, do not speak in such a fashion. You seem to be trying to invite yourself, which is not at all the thing," said Lady Adelaide. "It is too coming, you see."

Diana gave her a dark look.

"Miss Leigh, if you were able to attend, I would be delighted. Perhaps Sarratt would care to come as well, for he has an ear for music, I believe. Lady Adelaide, of course, you would be most welcome."

Promises were made, and leaves taken, Lady Adelaide continuing on down the street, followed behind at respectful distance by Mitzi, her maid. Diana wondered idly if Lady Adelaide was aware, as she was, that Mitzi hailed not from Paris but from Gloucestershire.

After a short, but mutually pleasing conversation about the merits of Albinoni versus Handel, Diana indicated to the earl that it was time she must return home. Helping her up into her carriage, it was then that Lord Weymouth noticed, for the very first time, that Sarratt's ward was becoming a very attractive young lady.

Chapter 17

The Duke of Sarratt had finished his agricultural discussions with the Broadbrooke tenants early on in his stay in the country, but he made no move to return to town. The business to be conducted during the trip, while useful, had been by no means of a critical nature; rather, it had been designed with the particular intent of providing for him as many hours of reflection as might be required to settle his uneasy mind and bring it back into a state of relative peace.

His grace spent long hours pacing up and down the galleries at Broadbrooke, the sounds from his highly polished Hessian boots shrilly echoing off the long, empty marble hallways. In those settings, the duke contemplated the various representations of his ancestors: many portrayed in paintings of family groups, and a few petrified in alabaster busts. In particular, he paid attention to portraits and statues of his own father, Edward Wellesford, 5th Duke of Sarratt, a near likeness, and one which served to bring the person himself vividly to mind.

Charles Wellesford had not liked his father above half. He considered him both profligate and promiscuous, and he never forgave the man for giving in to either weakness. Truth be told, Charles could not wait to get his own hands on the estates, in order to foster them and improve them, even though he knew this circumstance could only come about by means of his father's death. It was not that he had wished his father dead, for he had not; he had only wanted the welfare of the Wellesford family and their many tenants to be quickly placed into wiser and more conservative hands, which he believed his own to be.

What had brought him out to contemplate his destiny at Broadbrooke was the decision he knew he must carry out with haste: to marry at once a girl of good family, and put all thoughts of the serving-girl out of his mind forever.

His reflections in the country made him well aware of the trouble he had made for himself. He had wanted to take her as his mistress, she had refused him, and he was desperately angry with her for rejecting him and deceiving him.

But it was not so very easy to say to himself, "Give her up." Beyond the strong surge of passionate attraction that he had on first sight of her, a lingering fondness, a tenderness toward the girl had arisen in him, despite her rejection of his perfectly legitimate offer. There was in him a fondness and tenderness toward her—it was quite unwished for; it was undesired and undesirable.

Upon reflection, he knew that he had the very warmest feelings toward her, feelings that had never occurred toward any other woman in his life. More to the point, he was infatuated with the girl.

What did that mean? It meant that her image possessed him, day and night. She was always present to him, in thought or as a vision arising in his mind. There only had to be a single strong thought of her passing through, and his heart would catch and his breath quicken.

What was happening to him?

Was it illness? Was it witchcraft? Was he possessed by her? Why had she not accepted him? Why had his good offer made her so angry?

These were the questions he had to address before returning to town and offering for Lady Adelaide Hench-art's hand.

It seemed to him, depressingly enough, that above all other possibilities, it was most likely that his father's propensities were coming to the fore in him at last. The maid, Mary, was a pretty woman, nay, an extraordinary woman—but she was a woman of common birth. Even if her father had really been a deacon—which, after what Weymouth had said, he was very much inclined to doubt—in looks, she was of the same sort his father had spent thousands of guineas on at Rundell and Bridge's. Why would she be the one female to first set his heart racing, save that he had inherited from his father not only his vast estates, but his vast weaknesses? It was a lowering thought.

What was worse was finding the solution to it. Developing late in life, as he obviously had, a taste for the company of low-born women, ought he to marry at all? Would he then ignore his wife as his father had ignored his own mother? Or, knowing that his would be a marriage of convenience, such as persons of his rank customarily undertook, should he freely do as so many others had done—marry high and well-born, while indulging his heart in romances with the low? Was it a case of having his cake and eating it, too?

In the end, after much reflection, he decided that sober discipline was the order of the day.

He *would* make the offer for Lady Adelaide's hand in

marriage, and do so within the week. He also decided that Mary, his beautiful, troubling, troublesome female servant, must be dismissed, instantly, upon his return to town.

Her rejection of his offer of *carte blanche* he put down to naivete, rather than greed, as he had first supposed it. It was obvious the girl did not know her place.

Chapter 18

The duke returned to Sarratt House on a Sunday evening, and was welcomed warmly at dinner by his mother, who was in particularly high spirits, and by his ward Diana Leigh, whose countenance and manner had changed so drastically in the time he had been at Broadbrooke that, had he met her at a ball or the theater, he would not have known it was the same young girl.

He stared at the girl, who was the orphaned daughter of Viscount Steele, and realized that she finally had begun to resemble her late father. Her sallow hair had been brightened; her posture was almost elegant, almost assured. Her tone, rather than being sullen and petulant, had become confident, gracious, and welcoming. Her complexion was bright and even, and her mood was as high as he had ever seen it. A veritable miracle had been wrought: the ugly duckling had been transformed into the swan.

"Diana, you are in very good looks tonight," said her guardian, with pride. "Your appearance, your carriage, your demeanor are suddenly that of a perfect young lady. You seem suddenly to have become quite grown up."

"She has been working very hard all this week, you must know, and I think all the changes Diana has made are very becoming," said his mother.

"Do you really think I am improving, Uncle Charles?"

"I do, indeed. You are looking splendid. I congratulate you."

"Do you think I will do well this season?"

"I am sure of it, my dear."

"Charles, on that note, speaking of the season, while you were away Diana and I had occasion to go through her wardrobe and make a full reckoning of what clothing is suitable and what really must be bought. Shall we show you the list of items we wish to purchase? I must warn you that the charges will be considerable. There are gowns, and gloves, and really *everything* to be considered. Farley really had not been paying proper attention to what is, these days, required by a young girl in terms of a proper wardrobe."

"The money is of no consequence to me, provided that you yourself approve the quality and style of the purchases. One must regard the cost of a wardrobe suitable for cutting a dash in one's first season as being somewhat in the line of an investment, one intended to bring a considerable return."

"What return, Uncle Charles?" asked Diana, in all innocence.

The duke smiled broadly, saying, "Why, a brilliant marriage for the girl in question."

"Uncle Charles! Don't make me blush!"

"High color suits you, my dear. As does your new style of hair, and—really, so many things about you have been altered slightly, or heightened, all for the better—I am quite in awe. You have the look of your father about you now. I am curious as to what has wrought these changes. What can have inspired you so?"

"It's all due to Mary, Uncle Charles."

Instantly on the alert, the duke's face became imperceptibly harder.

"Mary? What 'Mary'?"

"The maid, Charles, the new one who had that funny altercation with Lady Adelaide on the stairs some time past," said his mother. "Don't you recall? A very pretty thing with black hair, deep blue-violet eyes—you must recall her! The one who had trouble with the landing-door. I had a little talk with Buckley, and he suggested that we move the girl upstairs. She's respectable, very clean, has excellent manners, and she even reads to me in the evenings. For Diana never has the time, and Farley cannot read of course, and my eyes have grown so weak of late. Isn't it a remarkable change for the better? Buckley reminded me that Diana was ready to have a personal maid to serve her, and we both thought that this Mary would do very well. As you see, it has all turned out really brilliantly."

"No. I'm sorry, but I won't have it."

"Uncle Charles, what can you mean?"

"I mean that I won't have that girl working upstairs among the family."

"Charles, why *ever* not?"

The duke was hard put to answer this question, for it was not the girl's conduct he was afraid would be unseemly, but his own. He knew he was being unfair, and irrational, but the truth was, he feared the girl with the violet eyes—feared the power she possessed with regard to him. The duke now viewed her very presence as a danger to his resolve to do his duty, wanted her out of his sight, and out of his mind—forever.

"Why not? Well, she's clumsy, for one thing," he ventured. "Look what a mess she made of Adelaide's dress. And that tea set can't be replaced a penny a dozen, can it?"

"Clumsy, is she? Well, her position no longer requires her to be carrying anything, much less anything so very heavy as a silver tray and tea set. What work she's doing now, she does excellently well. You can see for yourself what a change she's brought in Diana. You really must give her a chance. Mary's a very taking little thing, and I must say that I enjoy her company myself."

"No, Mother, it's out of the question. Diana must have a proper maid, a French maid, not some—refugee come up from the cellars. Furthermore, I want that Mary sent away—and I want it done tonight. Have Buckley come to me after dinner."

"But what has she done?"

"She hasn't done anything."

"Then why should she go?"

"Because I wish it! She's just not suitable. Surely you must see that," said the duke with asperity, wishing the conversation to a swift end.

"You seem very oddly prejudiced against her, Charles," said his mother. "I wish you would explain this sudden aversion to me, for I don't see how or why it has arisen."

"This is my house, and I shall be the judge of who belongs here. The girl goes, and she goes at once."

"Uncle Charles! No, it's not fair! You can't do this to me!" cried Diana.

"Moderate your tone at once, young lady," said her guardian, "or I'll send you to your room. What can you be thinking of, to behave toward me in this unseemly manner?"

Diana pushed her chair back, slapped her napkin down on the table, burst into tears, and ran out of the room.

crying, "Now that Mary has come to me, for the very first time in my entire life, I am beginning to look like a lady, and act like a lady. I *need* her. I *need* to have Mary with me. She helps me to feel that I have some beauty, some worth, all my own, in my own right, not just because people know I'm an heiress!

"Can't you understand that I need her? Why must you be so prejudiced against her? What has *she* ever done to you? I hate you, Uncle Charles! I hate you! I hate you!"

As she slammed the door shut, there was a moment of shocked silence before the duke added, pointedly, "Well, if *that* little display of temper is due to her new abigail's influence, I think my case against the girl is fully proven."

"Really, I think you must be ill, Charles," said the dowager in an irritated tone. "I do not condone Diana's behavior, for it could not have been more immoderate, but I beg you will reconsider your decision about this girl."

"Not you, too, Mother?"

"Yes. Absolutely. Charles, I can't for the life of me think why you wish to interfere with the details of the running of the household. You certainly have never expressed any interest in staffing arrangements previously—why should you begin now, pray tell?"

"Mother, you should know that Weymouth was uneasy enough to have gone to the trouble of speaking to me on the subject; it is *not* the thing to have a girl of that sort of beauty working in a household. Disturbs the other servants he said, bad for staff morale, sort of thing that looks peculiar when one entertains guests. Bound to be questions, you see. Not the sort of girl one expects to see in service, that's all."

"That's hardly her fault, Charles."

"No, no, not the girl's fault, of course. That she looks as she does. Not at all."

"Certainly not. How unfair you are! Her actions have been perfectly modest, and I think Weymouth very old-fashioned in his ideas of domestic propriety. More to the point, Charles, the beneficial influence of this girl upon your ward, who spent most of the beginning of her London season weeping and miserable, has been incalculable. Somehow, Mary is succeeding in teaching her things that are vital to her social success, things such as we had hoped would come to her through Lady Adelaide. You cannot send her away. You must not—in fact, I will not allow you to do so. It would be terribly unfair to Diana."

The duke put down his napkin and pushed his chair back from the table. Wretched gift of circumstance, that he should be forced to keep Mary on.

"Oh, very well, Mother. Let it be just as you wish. I only hope we may not regret this rash, ill-considered decision in the future."

The dowager duchess looked with complete lack of understanding at her son, as he swirled his glass of port, looking dissatisfied. She thought his whole attitude very distressing. Why had he gone into the country so abruptly, in the middle of the season? Whatever was bothering him now?

Perhaps it was just a case of prenuptial nerves. With Lady Adelaide as his chosen, she could hardly blame her son for being out of sorts.

However, she had Diana's welfare to protect, and that welfare now depended upon young Mary Simpson staying on, not being dismissed through some antiquated notions of Lord Weymouth's and some inexplicable fit of nerves of her son's.

"Charles, if you're worried about her background, I'll tell you this much: I myself thought her an odd choice, when I had speech with her first, but for that very reason I had Buckley summon her and question her at length as to the details of her background. He informed me that she seems to be precisely what she says she is: literate, of decent birth, penniless, alone in London, much in need of a position."

"Penniless?" he asked, with a guilty glance at the thick gold band outlining the heirloom china that held the remains of his dinner. "Is she?"

"Of course she's penniless. She's a lower servant, Charles. Really, you can be most exasperatingly obtuse at times. She is penniless; she is also senior among her siblings, and quite desperate for work."

If she's penniless, then why did she refuse my offer of protection? Did she really expect me to marry her? Was she an innocent girl, with proper morals? Or was she trying to ensnare me by pretending to be so?

His grace had no idea what about Mary was true and what was untrue. He knew how he felt about her—he felt hopelessly attached to her. He wished her at Jericho, but it was clear this wish would not be granted him. Against his better judgment, against his will, he gave in.

"Well, then, if she's truly desperate, and works well for Diana, I suppose we can't just cast her out, can we?" he said softly, thus condemning himself to a most painful future.

"No. More to the point, one can't punish a girl for having been born looking like a goddess come to earth, Charles," said the dowager. "After all, it's not a crime."

Is it not? Then why has her terrible beauty begun to seem like such a punishment to me?

Chapter 19

Duncan Baker had been interrogating the staff at the Dunberton Inn for what seemed like the hundredth time, and he was fast losing his temper. Not using her real name, of course, he had already described Lady Mary Hamilton to the staff in detail. He mentioned her dark hair, her violet eyes, her fine complexion, all her unforgettable features, and, to each person he talked to, he gave a shilling to sweeten the pot and brighten their attitude. Nothing came of it.

He did the whole dance again twenty times, to the ostlers, the waiters, the barmaids, the innkeeper, the boots. No one, it seemed, had seen the dratted wench. The Dunberton Inn was the third place he'd tried, and he was beginning to lose hope.

Only the thought of the dressing down he would receive from Sir Barton Ayleston was enough to keep him at it. Duncan was just standing around the back door of the inn, wondering where to go next, when a young boy pulled up a cart at the door and hailed a kitchen maid.

"Here's your beer, then," he said cheerfully. "Let me help you to carry in the kegs."

"You're a good lad, there, Sam," said the girl. "Always helpful."

A thought occurred to Duncan Baker, and he acted upon it.

"Say, there, young lad. You come here every day, don't you?"

The young boy eyed him suspiciously.

"Who wants to know?"

Duncan took a shiny shilling out of his pocket and tossed into the air.

"I want to know," he said.

The boy took the shilling, bit it to see if it was real, and slipped it quickly into his pocket.

"What you want to know, then?" he asked the stranger.

"You come here every day, do you? And you know the people hereabouts?"

" 'Course I do. Take me for a flat? I know everyone for ten mile around here. I drive here from home four times a day, regular as clockwork, dawn to dusk."

"You ever seen a special girl here, a particular girl, a girl with violet eyes? Hair black as night? Would have been several weeks back? You'd remember her well, if you'd seen her. I'd pay well for anyone who could give me some good information about her."

The boy narrowed his eyes again as he measured up his customer.

"Maybe I has. An' maybe I hasn't," said the child.

Irked, Duncan took out another shilling and showed it to the boy. The boy shook his head. He took out a second shilling, and the boy just laughed. Finally, he took out a sovereign, which the child snatched away from him in an instant.

"Ah, that's the ticket, Guv. I seen her. I seen that girl.

Pretty as a picture, she was, and kindly, too. Manners of a lady of quality. Asked me if I could hide her in the straw, and drive her over to the Smithfield Road, on a lark. Nice young lady. Very willin' to talk, very willin' to laugh. Liked her."

"Where was she headed after that, can you tell me that, boy?"

The boy started to laugh, and made a sign with his thumb and first finger. Duncan looked around, saw no one in immediate sight, and picked the impertinent brat up by the collar.

"See here, brat! No more o' yer tricks, and no more o' my blunt. Where'd the chit go off to? Tell me now, or it'll be the worse for you."

"I won't tell you! An' my brother works round here, and he's big and rough, an' if he sees what yer doin', he'll be doin' it to you, too, so put me down, hear?"

Reluctantly, he did so.

"Now, pay up like a man, an' maybe I'll tell you what you wants to know."

Duncan counted out some coins, the boy grinned with triumph, and began to dance a little jig of happiness.

"Tell me, then, boy, or I'll box your ears whether your big brother is around to help you or not."

"Said she was catching the stagecoach. Goin' south."

"How far south?"

"M—maybe to London."

Duncan Baker, never a man of his word, boxed his ears smartly and let the boy go away howling. He went back inside the Dunberton Inn, very satisfied with himself. A good day's work it had been.

The old coot Ayleston was going to have to pay him handsomely before he would divulge this knowledge, and Duncan would enjoy very much the bargain session that was to come.

In celebration of his improving fortunes, Duncan treated himself to a pitcher of excellent ale. He paid his shot, and rode on back to Danby Court to deliver the welcome news.

Duncan Baker strode into Sir Barton Ayleston's library without announcement. He threw his gloves on an ormolu secretary, and his dusty ridingcoat on a satin-covered chair.

"I've found her," he said. "At least, I've found out which direction she's gone in."

Sir Barton's eyes glittered with excitement. He left his books for the moment, and went over to speak with his minion.

"Very good work, Duncan. Which way did she go?"

"I think we should discuss the details of my compensation, Sir Barton, before we discuss the details of my discovery."

Sir Barton, looking displeased, replied, "How much do you want?"

"Two thousand pounds," said Duncan Baker, trying to keep his voice from wavering as he divulged this exorbitant amount. "Cash money."

"Done!" said Sir Barton in an instant. He had been afraid Duncan would ask for far more, aware as he was of how desperately Sir Barton needed to recover the girl. "Now, where has she gone?"

"To London."

"Excellent news! Excellent intelligence!"

He rang for his man, and ordered that his nephew be found and brought down to them. Gervase arrived not long after, looking winded, as if he'd run all the way from the other wing of the house.

"Yes, Uncle? You called for me?" he asked.

"Gervase, why don't you go on down to London?" asked Sir Barton Ayleston smoothly.

"London, Uncle?"

"You've heard of it, then?"

Stung, Gervase made no reply. His uncle ignored him.

"Yes, London—Duncan here has had the excellent fortune to have discovered the girl has fled to the capital. What a surprising and feisty wench! Who would have thought the chit would have had such fire in her, to travel all that way by herself?"

"I consider it most immodest of the girl to have run off like that. I wonder if some persons may have taken advantage of her already."

"Oh, don't worry, Gervase. Even if someone has already taken advantage of her, I feel sure you will be able to take advantage of the girl again."

"Quite!"

"Take this miniature down to London, show it around freely, and make inquiries amongst the ton—beginning at the fringes, and working inwards, so as not to tip our hand."

"Very well, Uncle. I shall have Randall pack for me this evening, and I will be off at dawn."

"Good! This is very good news for us. If Lady Mary has gone off to London, it would explain many things. She must be hiding among the Upper Ten Thousand. What fun! Shouldn't be too hard to find a needle in *that* haystack, should it, Gervase?"

Chapter 20

The time that followed the duke's return from Broadbrooke passed quickly for the occupants of Sarratt House,
great and small. It was the height of the London season,
and everyone was occupied with the round of balls and
routs, and the morning-calls that followed. The duke was
called upon to escort his ward to Almack's, where, against
all expectations, the Hon. Diana Leigh did very well
indeed, attracting any number of suitable admirers. His
grace also escorted the Lady Adelaide Henchart to the
theater and to a number of fashionable private parties,
very faithfully and correctly.

It was very generally known, however, that he still
had not yet formally offered for her hand, and this was
beginning to cause talk. Would his grace ever come up
to scratch? Would he remain the ton's richest and most
eligible bachelor? The Hon. Lionel Fitzmartin and the Earl
of Weymouth had a huge wager riding on the outcome:
Fitzmartin betting that he would, in time, offer for the

girl, and Weymouth betting against it—the wager being to the tune of several thousand pounds.

The truth of the duke's dilemma was that the longer he spent time in Lady Adelaide's company, the less he wished to repeat the experience. Her laughter grated on his nerves, he found her opinions shallow at best and mean-spirited at worst; she appeared to think about nothing beyond procuring herself the most expensive adornments, and scheming about ways of inducing society to admire her. In short, she was abominable company.

And what of Mary, the girl who had refused to become his mistress? Day after day, he was forced to admit that he thought the behavior of a domestic far superior to the behavior of the woman he still intended to wed.

It was a very painful situation for him. Now Mary had become not just Diana's favorite confidante, but his mother's confidante; he had had to endure meeting the girl almost daily. Daily he underwent the humiliation of being in the presence of a woman he desperately wanted to possess, but could not approach, except dishonorably. Far from recovering from his infatuation with her, he was forced, day after day, to acknowledge the wide range of her good qualities: she obviously had instilled Diana with a sense of taste, of polish, of manners, and address. She tended to the needs of his mother as if she were her natural born daughter: she was always attentive, she did precisely as she was bid, she spent hours patiently reading whatever the dowager required.

The duke and Lady Mary had reached an unspoken agreement as to how they would conduct themselves in the face of the mutually embarrassing scene that had occurred between them. Their unspoken agreement was this: to pretend the scene had not occurred, the offer had never been made, never misunderstood, and never rejected. They behaved toward one another with the care-

ful propriety that was suitable to define the circumstance
of master and servant.

One day during this time, the Hon. Diana Leigh was
taking a brisk walk near the Serpentine, accompanied by
her abigail, Mary Simpson. Their appearance in the park
was now a very usual occurrence; anyone who wished to
meet Miss Leigh could easily encounter her.

It was with encountering her in mind that Lord Weymouth, riding with the Duke of Sarratt, had come to the
park. They greeted Diana, who inclined her head toward
them in return.

"Miss Leigh!" said Lord Weymouth. "I'm pleased to
meet you here, Miss Leigh. I had some matters about
which I wanted to seek your advice—would you care to
take a turn with me around the park?"

Diana, thrilled, accepted with alacrity and with a very
becoming blush.

After a moment, the two men dismounted. Weymouth
hailed two young boys, and gave them a coin to see that
their horses were walked until the men had need of them
again.

Lord Weymouth offered his arm to Diana for a turn
around the green. Diana, thrilled, accepted.

"Thank you, Lord Weymouth. Upon what do you need
my advice?"

"My cousin Dorothea, inspired by the example of Mae-
stro Waldner, wants to set up a gathering of friends who
play instruments. I think she would like it very much if
you would come, and perhaps give her your ideas as to
what pieces we might most successfully perform."

"That of course depends entirely upon the skills of the
players. Will you be joining in yourself, Lord Weymouth?"

"I am looking forward to it."

"Then I think we may attempt some more difficult pieces, since your playing is so very good."

"A mere amateur, I'm afraid."

The Duke of Sarratt had been walking next to Diana and Weymouth during this conversation, Mary following respectfully a few yards behind, when his grace realized that his presence was unnecessary to the conversation, indeed that he was somewhat in the way.

The duke fell behind also, and he and Mary, staying well apart, walked along for a good five minutes saying nothing at all. Weymouth and Diana were chattering on in rapt conversation about Hayden and Handel, quite unaware of anyone else but themselves.

The duke, uneasy at being alone with Mary for the first time since he had been foolish enough to offer to keep her, hoped that silence would be enough to shield him from the temptation of discourse by her exquisite presence. He hoped against hope that Weymouth would finish chatting up his ward and return to his side.

Mary, painfully aware that the last time she had been alone with this man he had made her an immoral offer, was nearly out of her mind. She wanted to run away from him; she wanted to scream; she wanted to weep; she wanted to strike him once again.

Instead, trying to rid herself of this sense of unease, she blurted out a question:

"Lord Weymouth seems to admire your ward, does he not, your grace?"

This, to the duke whose manly pride had been injured, was a piece of impertinence, and the last straw. He felt actually glad of an occasion to depress the chit's pretensions once and for all. Drawing himself up to his full height, which was considerable, the duke gave Mary a cold quelling look that she shrank from.

He removed his quizzing-glass from his pocket, which he rarely used, and stared at Mary slowly from top to toe, his lip curling slightly in an unaccustomed sneer.

"Whatever may have passed between us once in private, my girl, you are not to address me in public," said the duke with cruel precision. "I see I must remind you of your position: you are nothing but my ward's dressingroom maid.

"While Diana may unwisely allow you some latitude in *her* conversations with you, you are *not* to assume that allows you leave to converse with *me* on such free and familiar terms, or, indeed, with any of your betters.

"I beg you: do not forget yourself. I know not the true particulars of your so-called 'upbringing,' nor the real reason you do not quite fit in either upstairs or downstairs. I do know that we all occupy our respective places in society, having been placed there by the will of the divine. One must become used to that, and not trespass between classes. To ignore this natural ranking, to ape one's betters, to seek to insinuate oneself into another social circumstance, is to face inevitably evil consequences. I beg you will keep that in mind."

Stung by his words, humiliated beyond belief, tears slid down her face as she tried her hardest to keep her tongue—but it was not to be.

"What have I done to deserve such treatment at your hands?" she whispered back at him. "How *can* you speak to me so, sir?"

"Whyever should I not?" he said, in a low harsh tone. "Why do you *dare* to address me again, girl?"

"How can you be so cruel? Do you think that because I live in servitude, I have no feelings?"

"Your feelings," he said disparagingly, brushing a bit of lint off his coat, "the feelings of a *servant,* can be of no possible concern to me."

At this, the Lady Mary Hamilton then lost all semblance of self-control.

"Does your grace assume that I am lost to all qualities of humanity because I polish silver tea sets, rather than pour out tea from them? Am I lost to qualities of humanity because I mend the hems of gowns from Madame Fanchon's, rather than wear them? Have I lost all qualities of humanity because I tend to jewels, rather than adorn myself with them?"

The duke, shocked, stopped dead in his tracks as the girl went on.

"Once, long ago, I very much admired you for your character. Once, I considered you not merely a nobleman, I had thought you a man with a noble heart. I can see how wrong I was: you are as arrogant, prejudiced, vapid, and stupidly self-important as any other town-dandy. From the unbelievably arrogant, callous, immoral offer you once made me, to your imperious attempt to deal me a set-down today, you have wronged me, sir. I say again: you have wronged me.

"Yes, your grace, it *is* perfectly true: I am but your servant, an abigail, born so low I am not worthy of any offer *but* a base one," Mary went on, still in a fury. "Born so low that you quite reasonably expected I should have jumped at your kind offer of protection with joy and gratitude—for having condescended to deal so far beneath you as to have admitted your admiration of me!

"Very well! I am beneath you! I am a servant! I am your servant, your grace! But I say to you, your grace–hath not a servant eyes? Hath not a servant 'hands, organs, dimensions, senses, affections, passions,' as said the Bard of Avon? Are we servants not fed with food as you, can we not be 'hurt with the same weapons, subject to the same diseases, warmed and cooled by the same winter and summer. If you prick us, do we not bleed? If you poison us, do we not die?'"

There was another silence.

"Moreover, now that you have insulted me, for the second time, and tried to cut me to the quick, remembering what you said today, and how you said it, tell me: did *that* sneering manner of yours typify the civil address that is the hallmark of good breeding?

"Or is breeding one thing, and civility quite another? Is one required to be civil only to one's social peers?"

There was silence once again. Mary's eyes were wet with tears, which she tried desperately to choke back. She turned away from him and wiped her tears with her hands.

The duke suddenly felt ashamed—ashamed of his harsh words, and ashamed of his profound arrogance. His words had sprung from fear, for he feared himself, and he feared his feelings for Mary, which were quite beyond his control. Burdened by fear, he had struck out at her, hoping to free himself, hoping to regain control over his own heart.

It was clear to the Duke of Sarratt that he had accomplished just the opposite: he knew just at that moment that all was lost, for he had begun to move beyond passion and attachment toward her. He had begun to love her, though he dared not say so.

He followed her, wanting to feel her presence near to him. Still angry, she turned away from him again, but he followed her again, and she stopped.

Standing directly behind her, close enough to Lady Mary that she trembled, the duke spoke, this time in a voice as deep and soft as velvet, his lips only inches from her ear.

"Mary, please listen to me: I apologize for what I said. I didn't mean a word of what I said, not any of it. It was unforgivably rude of me. I am so very sorry."

Still offended, she said, stiffly, "I am sorry, too. I should not have spoken to you without your leave, sir."

"I am ashamed to have suggested as much. There are certain—certain reasons for my behavior which I cannot at this time express. I beg you will forgive me. Be kind enough not to judge my character by this episode alone."

Lady Mary looked directly at the duke for what seemed a long time, and she saw that he was speaking from his heart. Moved, she replied, "I shall not, your grace."

He offered her his handkerchief to blot her tears, which she gratefully accepted.

Then, keeping a discreet distance apart, they walked on together, shadowing the steps of Lord Weymouth and Diana. Soon they began to converse with one another, at first tentatively, shyly, but quickly gaining confidence and speaking more freely, taking pleasure in one another's nearness. They chose neutral topics, such as the weather, and farming, and fashion, and literature.

They walked on for a bit, and then the duke laughed to himself, briefly.

"What amuses you?" asked Mary.

"Something just occurred to me: I have just realized that during your extremely moving recitation of Shakespeare a few minutes past, you omitted a line. Why was that?"

"Oh, I thought it impolitic to mention that line about how 'if we are wronged, do not we too seek revenge?' It was, under the circumstances, too provocative."

He laughed again. "What a diplomat you are! No, actually I was thinking of a line before that: I believe it goes: 'If you prick us, do we not bleed? If you tickle us, do we not laugh?'"

"One can easily understand that: I omitted the line about tickling, because I was afraid it would ruin the dignity of my presentation. I might have giggled, you see."

They fell into a mutual silence again. At one point the duke stopped walking, and turned to her.

"Mary, though I am the master, and you the servant, will you consent to be my friend?"

"Yes, your grace," said Lady Mary. "Certainly."

The couple continued on, still following Lord Weymouth and Diana Leigh. At a certain point they stopped, and allowed themselves to look at one another. They stayed there for a moment, transfixed, until they heard the vague sound of an approaching carriage. From a distance, as if in a far-off dream, they heard the duke being hailed by someone: it was Lady Adelaide Henchart.

"Hullo, Duke!" she called to him.

His grace did not at once reply, but suddenly backed away from Mary, shattering their mutual reverie, bringing them back to the ordinary world once more.

"Adelaide, did you see what just happened? Did you see the two of them springing apart just now? How singular," said her brother, gesturing toward Sarratt.

"Two of whom?"

"Sarratt and that girl over there. She's very beautiful, isn't she? Stunning face, really stunning. Lovely figure; exquisite eyes. Bad gown, though. Who do you suppose she is? Does Sarratt keep ladybirds?"

"I don't think he approves of them. I can't imagine who it might be; I know everyone there is to know, and I can't say I recognize her. I can't quite see from here—wait till we are closer. Oh, no, Roger—it's that dreadful maid of theirs! I told you about what she did to me, didn't I? What can he be thinking of, to be seen with her in public? What is she doing out of the house? I must know."

"She's a breathtaking armful, that's what. That's why he wants to be seen with her. I'd wager she gets him to *her* bed before *you* get him to the altar."

"That's not amusing, Roger."

"Wasn't meant to be. I think it's true. He appears to be utterly infatuated by her, if I know anything about the subject, which I do."

Lady Adelaide Henchart snapped her parasol shut.

"When I am the Duchess of Sarratt, Roger, I will remember your continual impertinences, and it will only make me counsel my husband to keep his purse-strings tied shut tight against you."

"Come down off your high horse, Adelaide. Do you think it an insult if I mention Sarratt's having a fancy piece? Don't be fustian."

"I'm sure I don't care at all what the man does in his leisure hours," she said with a sniff.

"So long as he marries you?" said her brother, a smile on his face.

"Well, yes," she admitted, "Just so."

By the time Lady Adelaide Henchart had arrived in the spot where her friends were, and been handed down from the barouche by her brother, Lady Mary Hamilton had contrived to drift off from the place where the quality was standing. She had very deliberately placed herself off to the side, some yards from her mistress, who had ended her walk with the Earl of Weymouth. That couple was standing under a tree, talking animatedly about some quartet by Handel that they hoped to play together.

Lady Adelaide advanced upon the Duke of Sarratt, and began to engage him in a light conversation, which his grace attempted to endure as best he could. He found it particularly painful to be required to attend solely to her insipid remarks, while forced by the conventions of society to ignore the existence of Mary altogether.

Roger Henchart, having nothing better to do with himself, decided he would have a word with the duke's pretty maid, and made his way over to her.

"Girl!" he said to her with an ingratiating smile.

"Sir?" she answered, not sure of who was addressing her, never having seen Roger Henchart before.

"What is your business here?"

"Why do you ask, sir?" replied Mary, in her dignified way.

"Don't be impertinent. Why were you talking with the duke just now?"

Mary wondered why this man, who had obviously arrived with Lady Adelaide Henchart, was addressing her in this imperious way. Gentlemen of quality did not, as a general rule, speak with servants, unless there was some very particular reason for so doing.

"His grace was speaking to me, sir. I merely answered him."

"What did he say?"

"You must ask his grace that, sir. I must go: my mistress calls me."

"Your mistress calls you?" said Roger in a lightly mocking tone.

"Yes," she said, wishing for a moment that she had not placed herself quite so far from the two couples.

"What a coincidence. Your mistress calls you, yet *I* would call *you* 'mistress,'" he whispered seductively.

"Pardon?" said Mary, backing away from him, unable to believe her ears.

"I *said,* I would call you my mistress, girl," he said silkily, backing her against a tree and tipping her chin up with his hand. "Would you not care for that? I think you would find such an arrangement pleasurable—and I would make it well worth your while. It was never said of me that I was tight-fisted when confronted by true beauty, such as yours.

"Well, girl, what say you? Shall I settle you in a love-nest on Thurber Street? I'll give you everything you wish for in the world!"

How could this be happening again? Lady Mary wondered with horror. Was it only that gentlemen had to cast their eyes upon her face, and thoughts of ways to dishonor her would arise? Had she somehow led him to believe his obnoxious attentions would be welcomed?

"Never speak to me in that familiar way again," she snapped, ducking beneath his arms, and turning away from him.

"Who do you think you are, chit?" he said angrily, taking hold of her wrist, as she tried to walk off, and holding her tightly. "How dare you use that tone of voice and attempt to dismiss me, as if I were trying to take liberties with a lady of quality. Don't put on airs with me, for I know you for what you are, doxy."

"Let me go!" she whispered, and twisted her wrist away from him.

She fairly ran back to her mistress. Her face was red with outrage, and she sent a fierce glance toward the duke that went unseen by him, but was seen by Lady Adelaide.

Lady Adelaide studied Mary's face, and wondered why she looked upset. She looked at her brother, who, on the other hand, was looking perfectly composed. He was strolling aimlessly about the grass, pretending nothing was amiss.

It was clear to her that Roger had been up to his old tricks again, which, as regarded Mary, did not displease her at all. A slip on the shoulder from Roger would surely sink the chit in Sarratt's eyes.

With this in mind, she said to her companion, "By the

way, that dreadful little maid of yours, Duke—why is she here? I meant to ask you."

"She is Diana's abigail now," said his grace carefully.

"What a disaster! I met Diana on the street with her some time ago, but I hoped she had by now come to her senses and found someone more suitable."

"Why so?"

"Well, Duke, one need only lay eyes on her to know: with those looks, I'm sure she's no better than she should be."

"She's perfectly respectable," said the duke, displeased.

"How would you know?"

"I—I had it looked into."

"You see? You must have had doubts about her yourself, or you wouldn't have had that done."

"She's a deacon's daughter," said Sarratt, wishing the interview to end.

"Nonsense! You don't really mean to tell me you've fallen for a story like that. Is there any proof? No, it's just the story the girl is putting about to make herself look respectable and insinuate herself into your household, and, by the look of things, she's doing a very good job of it, too. From housemaid to lady's maid in a fortnight! It's trickery, Charles, and I warn you of it now. Any girl who looks like that is ripe for—excuse my indelicacy," Lady Adelaide whispered, "Is ripe for a slip on the shoulder. Sooner or later she'll fall in the family way, and have to be turned out."

"That's very unkind, Adelaide, and I wish you will turn the subject at once."

"Perhaps it's unkind, but it's true!"

"What? Is it true that, simply because she's beautiful, and she's a servant, she must needs lack morals? No, Adelaide, any doubts that I had about her have long since been put to rest. Besides, she has been very good for Diana. Don't you think Diana seems much improved? Weymouth thinks so. He used to treat her a like a little sister, and now look at him—he can't seem to spend enough time with her. This from a man who has escaped the snares of females for as long as I have. I think Diana's transformation has been nothing short of miraculous. Do you not agree?"

"By no means. As to some improvement in her complexion, well, that maid's most likely been pushing Diana to use a rouge-pot; nothing could be more unfortunate for a girl in her first season, believe me. Think if she talks Diana into using those deadly cosmetics, the ones that whiten one's complexion at the risk of death. One cannot bear the responsibility for it. Won't you take my sincere advice and dismiss her?"

"No," said the duke with finality.

"Why not?"

"You concern yourself unnecessarily in my domestic affairs, Adelaide," snapped the duke, keeping his temper with difficulty. "It is not a quality in you I would encourage."

Adelaide, stung, held her tongue.

She had come all too close to having an altercation with Sarratt, which would have been a fatal error, and it was all the fault of that vulgar, scheming little maid.

Chapter 21

The duke spent the rest of that interminable day with Lady Adelaide Henchart, only escaping in the late afternoon, when she was forced to return home to dress for her evening's engagements. She pressed his hand meaningfully as they parted; the duke felt ill and out of sorts, and his grace retired to his library for the remainder of the day.

The Duke of Sarratt did not dine at home that night, but went to Brook's, where he hoped to be able to seek the counsel of his friends. He needed to unburden himself to one he trusted.

Making inquiries, he found that the Hon. Lionel Fitzmartin had gone suddenly into the country, and so he was doubly thankful when the Earl of Weymouth finally strolled in.

"Weymouth! I need to speak with you. Can we find a private corner?"

"Certainly. Is something amiss?"

"James, I hardly know how to begin. I'm—entangled.

I'm . . ." the duke's voice trailed off, for he was unable to go on.

"Do I apprehend that we are talking about a female, Sarratt? Or females?" asked Lord Weymouth.

"Yes," admitted the duke.

Lord Weymouth clapped his hands together and whooped with laughter.

"Excellent! It's the end of the world; hell has finally frozen over; I fully expect the resurrection next. The day the perpetually secretive, woman-hating Duke of Sarratt comes to me openly admitting he's having female troubles, my good fellow, *anything* can happen."

"I will you to stop quizzing me, man—it's not a laughing matter."

Wiping the tears from his eyes, Weymouth said, "To be sure it's not. Forgive me, but it's quite out of character for you. Tell me—who is she? Or who are they? It's not that servant of yours again, I hope?"

"Yes," said the duke ruefully. "The problem concerns her—and Lady Adelaide."

"I see. Famous! A case of heaven and hell, eh?"

The duke took a pull of brandy, took a deep breath, and launched into a recital of his troubles. He expressed his intense attraction toward Mary Simpson, his utter lack of attraction for Lady Adelaide Henchart, and he laid the matter out in its miserable entirety, hoping against hope his friend could find a solution for what seemed to him an insoluble problem.

"Knew you were in for deep trouble with that pretty little girl when I saw you together in your library. Never seen a look like that on your face in all my life. Very touching, indeed it was. But, you will recall, I told you then that the girl would cause you trouble. Told you then you were obsessed with her. Told you then you and

Adelaide don't suit: *that's* the crux of the dilemma right there.

"You don't like Adelaide above half, and by comparison, this pretty chit seems like an angel sent from heaven that you're in love with. Who knows? Perhaps you really *do* love her—happens all the time. Happens to the best of men—think about Fox and that boozy woman he lived with for so long—devoted couple. Living with a gal one loves can be a very good thing."

Lord Weymouth, who had a real regard for his oldest friend, chose his next words very carefully.

"But you can't *marry* the chit, old man," he said softly.

"Can't I?" said the Duke of Sarratt, looking up at the earl with a hopeless expression. "Fox wed his woman, after all, in the end."

Lord Weymouth replied with a slow and firm shake of his head.

"Fox weren't Duke of Sarratt. It won't do for you, not at all. Not the thing. Not done, old man."

"Elizabeth Gunning," his grace pointed out petulantly, "married not one duke, but *two* dukes."

"In succession, man! Beside, that was seventy years ago! The Gunning girl was penniless, but she was from Castle Coote; she wasn't just somebody's housemaid, laying down druggets and holland covers. No, it just won't do."

"I know," said the duke gloomily.

"Have to marry Adelaide. Better just do it, and get the thing over with. Good as pledged to her already. Said you two wouldn't suit, I know I did, but I was wrong: didn't know you were in love. If you're in love, you may as well marry Adelaide. She won't care about your being in love one way or another. Don't matter one whit to her. You can deal with the other one after you're leg-shackled."

"I suppose so."

"Can't be helped, old man. Family name—have to have a care for it. Can't marry just anybody, just because you're fond of her."

"I love her, Weymouth."

"Can't be helped. Rotten luck."

"After all this time . . . it seems so unfair."

He moved over to his great leather chair, sat down on it, and put his head in his hands. His friend watched him sympathetically, unsure how best to console him.

"It is unfair. Way of the world. Best just get it over with."

"You're right, of course," replied the duke.

"Forget about the girl for the time being. Stay at my place for a few days, why don't you? Out of sight, out of mind, sort of thing."

"I've tried that before. It doesn't fadge. I'd like to stay the night if I may; we're having Adelaide's family to dinner tomorrow, you recall. You'll be there, I trust?"

"With pleasure. Whatever I can do for you, I'll do. Just keep away from the pretty chit and you'll find your feelings fade away. Can't be real love, old boy; perhaps it's simply passion. You'll get over it—or perhaps you can try once again to make an arrangement with her."

"She doesn't seem to be that kind of girl."

"Be sensible, Charles. What other kind of girl can she be?"

The next morning, Lord Weymouth came to Sarratt House, in order to take Diana out for a drive in the park. Just as Diana was about to leave, she discovered a small tear in the hem of her skirt, and returned upstairs to have Mary sew it up again.

On her hands and knees, Mary sewed it with her deft, invisible stitches. Diana thanked her and dismissed her, and Mary returned downstairs to the servants' hall, where she had volunteered to help with darning the fine linens. Her stitchery being so fine, it was in great demand. The other maids were very grateful she did not consider such a task beneath her, now that she was serving Miss Diana.

Meanwhile, upstairs in her bedchamber, just as the duke's ward was picking up her white gloves, ready to go down once more, Diana noticed that something had been left on the carpet, rather near the spot where Mary had been sewing up the tear on the hem. She went closer to the object: it was a thin white satin riband, one which she recognized. The riband was one that her abigail habitually wore around her neck.

She picked it up, and in doing so saw a second object: knotted into the riband there was a golden ring, with a dark red jewel.

Diana Leigh looked the thing over with interest and surprise, and some considerable alarm. How could this ring possibly belong to Mary? It appeared to be made of pure gold, and bore an intricate crest with a lion rampant and a *fleur de lis*. The stone set in it was a dark pigeon's-blood red; it looked for all the world like a ruby, but how could that be?

Aware that Lord Weymouth disliked it when she was late, she nevertheless ran across to the duchess's sitting-room, knocked on the door, and went in.

"Nana, I have found something. Would you look at this ring, please?"

"Where did you get that, child?" asked the dowager, turning the ornament over, inspecting it closely.

"I found it on the floor of my bedroom. I think it belongs to Mary, for she wore something heavy on this riband. But see the ring—it looks like a ruby, doesn't it?"

"It does indeed."

"But how would Mary get a ruby ring? It's not one of ours, is it? I mean, I don't want to be rude, but, she hasn't stolen it from us, or something, has she?"

"No, it's not one of ours," said the dowager. "I know all of our pieces very well, and have catalogued them. However, this *does* appear to be genuine."

"How do you suppose that she got it?"

"I can't imagine, Diana."

"In any case, I must be off! Lord Weymouth is waiting to take me out, and I really must go to him! Would you think it over, and let me know what I must do about it? Or perhaps Buckley should be told? Dear me—I'll never be good at things like sorting out the servants. I don't know how I shall ever be able to manage a household of my own. I haven't the patience."

"Run along, child. I'll take care of it."

The dowager stared at the ring for a very long time. The coat of arms certainly appears familiar to me, she thought, but just where have I seen it before?

Her grace moved gracefully to her writing desk, and pulled out some paper.

Putting the signet ring on her desk, the dowager duchess very carefully began to sketch the ring, placing particular emphasis upon the crest. A *fleur de lis?* Why? Whose ring was this? From which family had it come, and why? Such things could be traced.

Then she took a second piece of paper from the desk and began writing on it. She placed both notes together, sealed them with a wafer, and pulled the bell for the footman.

Her grace hoped the mystery of the ring's provenance could be solved without any scandal, but it seemed unlikely. She pulled the bell again, and when Farley came in, she asked that Mary be sent to her at once.

* * *

"Mary, I have a question for you. Just what is this, please?"

In the small hand of the Dowager Duchess of Sarratt, Lady Mary saw her father's ruby signet ring. She gasped aloud, and paled. She tried to keep herself from trembling, but she could not. She only stared and stared at that treacherous ruby ring.

"Diana found this ring on the floor of her room," the duchess continued. "Because of the white riband that was with it, she told me that she believes that it may be yours. Is it yours, Mary?"

What was she to do? There could be no possible reasonable explanation for her having such a priceless thing in her possession. Should she admit it was hers? Her whole tale was entirely preposterous, who would believe her? Certainly not a woman as intelligent as the dowager, not for a moment. The duchess would call the authorities, and she'd be clapped into jail. The only way she would get out would be to call upon her stepfather, and then she'd pay an even worse price for freedom.

Should she simply deny that the ring was hers? How could she do so? Who would believe such a thing?

A whirl of contradictory thoughts invaded her consciousness, but in the end, she knew first, that she had to have the ring back, and second, that she could not possibly deny that it was hers.

Lady Mary tried to be brave, and face the situation squarely.

"Yes, the ring belongs to me, your grace," she said softly. "May I have it back now, please?"

The dowager, regarding her carefully, at first made no motion to return the ring. She then handed Mary both the riband and the ring, and she watched as Mary threaded the riband through it and placed it back upon her neck, not offering any further explanation.

There was a very uncomfortable silence before the duchess spoke, saying, in a cold tone, "Mary, I think you should tell me what this is all about. Can you bring yourself to do that?"

Mary's heart sank, as she replied, "No, ma'am, I can't tell you anything at all about it. I must not. I can only ask you to trust me. I came by the ring honestly, I swear it. Someone close to me gave it to me for safekeeping. I didn't steal it. I know it doesn't seem possible, but will you please, please try to trust me, and not turn me out of the house?"

The dowager duchess pursed her lips, weighing her options.

"Very well, Mary. I will give you this chance, and this chance only. Take a bit of time, and see if you can bring yourself to share your secret with me. I really cannot have someone in service here who is continually attracting suspicion to themselves as you seem to. This is the second time I have had to inquire as to your background. Make no mistake: you know you are withholding something from me, and so do I.

"As I have always liked you, and I certainly wish you well, I ask that you consider your situation very carefully. Anyone else would have told you to pack your bags and go away long since, but I like what you have done on behalf of Diana, and I have always liked your manner. I am prepared to give you the benefit of the doubt.

"I cannot, however, tolerate a servant who cannot bring herself to be candid with me. If you came by that ring honestly, you must tell me very precisely *how* you came to do so. I will give you some time to think the matter over. Then, if you cannot confide the truth to me by tomorrow morning, you must pack your things and leave this house at once."

"Yes, your grace."

Lady Mary Hamilton left the room feeling as though her very life were being crushed out of her. Why did that have to happen, now, of all times, when there were only a few days left? Could she run away? London wasn't safe for a young girl alone, and now she had no Fanny Simpson to act as her guardian and her chaperone. How could she leave the house? How could she stay on at Sarratt House without revealing everything she had sacrificed so much to conceal?

Chapter 22

"Damn the luck!" cried Gervase, throwing in his cards.
⟩u'd think I would be able to turn something to my
antage, but it's not to be tonight, I think."

Ie left the table, and strolled aimlessly through
lame Roland's parlor, looking over the shoulders of
⟩r players, thereby causing them to hold their cards
⟩e to their chests, and glare at him for his fecklessness.
'ollowing the information gained by Duncan Baker,
vase Ayleston had come all the way to London from
⟩by Court, but he was not having a very pleasant time
t. For one thing, his damnably tight-fisted uncle hadn't
⟩n him sufficient funds to enjoy the many pleasures
London life offered a young man on the town for
very first time. One wanted to enjoy oneself, after all;
wanted to kick up one's heels a bit.

⟩bove all, one wanted to make purchases: there was
excellent bay mare he'd seen at Tatt's. Gervase would
⟩e killed to own that prime bit of blood and bone, but
⟩ad no possible way of paying for her. He was reduced

merely to staring longingly at the animal, like a cl
looking in at a candy shop window. Really, it was gall

Another thing that upset him to no end was the wor
of the *demi-monde:* they were very amiable, and also v
expensive. In fact, they were only interested in how m
blunt he had to throw around, buying them trinkets; w
it became clear that he was just a young lad without fu
of his own, the luscious ladies withdrew their interest
set their caps at fatter prey with fatter purses. It was v
unfair.

It wasn't as if Sir Barton hadn't the funds, after all.
executor of his late wife's estate, he had access to fu
that Gervase could only dream of. His uncle could h
funded him and done so generously, but no, Uncle
never like that. Always counting the pennies. Sir Ba
had given him funds to carry out his plans in Lonc
but would want a full and complete accounting of th
tomorrow morning when he arrived in town.

Dismally, Gervase considered running off with
funds and spending the money just as he wished, but
knew he could never do it: he had not the backbone
withstand the uproar that such egregious disobedie
would cause. He thought of borrowing from the cent
cents, but discarded this idea as well.

It was better as it was. A bit of gaming he could affe
and he did that, hanging out in gaming-halls, playing
few hands he could, and making himself miserable v
feelings of envy mixed with martyrdom.

Gervase consoled himself with the thought that, if
girl was found in time—no, one should always try
look positively on the future—when the girl was fou
when she had become his wife and her fortune had pas
into his own hands, then there would be plenty of t
and plenty of blunt for fast horses, fast women, and

cey things that showed them off to best advantage.
er all this hard work, he felt he deserved better.

He found a seat at an empty table, and signaled for
ne port. He drank it reflectively; it was probably time
get down to business for the evening. God, he hated
s part of it; it made him feel so intrusive. There was
aply no polite way to go up to a complete stranger,
I show a portrait to him, and ask after the woman. It
s so vulgar and coming; it was not done, and yet that
precisely what his uncle expected him to do.

He had been in London for a whole week already, with
luck at all. Gervase had shown the miniature to ticket
lers at the theater, to shopkeepers on Bond Street, to
haughty salespeople at Madame Vergere's, all with
result. No one had seen her.

He had had the brilliant notion to show her likeness
he proprietors of each one of the circulating libraries,
he knew she was something of a bluestocking. He
s shocked when they, too, said they had never seen

There was one woman, a milliner, who thought she
ght have seen someone like her buying hats—but the
l wasn't really sure, and then she said it was not possible
t she could be a regular customer, for then her name
uld be known.

Now, there was nothing left for him to do but approach
quality directly, starting at its lower edges, which is
y he had come to Madame Roland's. It was unthinkable
show a picture around at Almack's, even had he been
e to obtain vouchers, which he thought he could not.
t at Madame Roland's one could find peers who were
ll in their cups, and who could perhaps answer an
pertinent question they would never answer when
per.

He had asked. Have you seen this girl? Do you recc nize this face?

He had been asking, and he had learned nothing of h

Though London was so large, the polite world was n This is what most distressed Gervase. If Lady Mary h been going out and about in the world—and why shou she not?—someone must have seen her.

Gervase was musing on this, wondering what to next, when a tall unknown man sat down next to hi They nodded to one another with a kind of lazy civil common to gentlemen of a certain class who have dru too much for their own good, and yet still are not sate

Gervase stared at Lady Mary's image for a mome wishing the girl to blazes for having caused him so mu trouble, and snapped the miniature shut.

"Forgive me, old man," said the stranger, who h watched this process with great interest. "That a frie of yours?"

Gervase became excited, but being less of a fool th his uncle thought, he was quick to disguise his exciteme since a casual manner was requisite in such delicate situ tions.

"She is someone I seek to find," he said with a frienc smile, opening the miniature again and showing it to t man. "You have not, by any chance, seen her?"

The Hon. Roger Henchart could hardly believe his luc It had been out all evening, but it seemed to be turni his way again. This young man, fashionably dressed, ob\ ously someone of quality, was looking for Sarratt's unwi ing little maid.

Now, Roger wondered why would that be, and ho could he turn it to his advantage? Perhaps the girl had be willing with someone else—with this young gentlema There was a mystery afoot. Surely he could find someo

ho would pay him to reveal a secret concerning—or to
eep it.

"Roger Henchart. Of Rutherfurd Manor."

"Ayleston. Gervase Ayleston."

"Of?"

"Danby Court."

"Can't say I know it."

"In Cumberland."

"You're a long way from home, then, man. What brings
ou all the way to London, Ayleston? Looking for that
irl?"

Gervase was taken aback, and stumbled in reply.

"No, no, I came on business. But I would like informa-
on about her. Do you have any? Have you seen her?"

"She looks quite familiar to me . . . but then, I really
an't be sure. What would you do with her if you found
er?"

How much could he reveal without tipping his hand,
Gervase wondered. It seemed like this dreadful fellow
as going to ask for a bribe. Probably a substantial one,
od rot him. In any event, his uncle was to join him on
he morrow—Uncle Barton would surely know how to
ort this business out—it was a relief finally to have
nformation to present to him. He desperately wanted this
whole matter closed and settled forever. Perhaps it didn't
natter how much it cost.

"There are certain—ah, delicate business questions I
would put to her," said Gervase. "About some—prop-
rty."

"I see. And the girl knows about this 'property'?"

"I—I believe she may know something," Gervase
eplied in a disinterested tone.

"And would the girl's whereabouts be worth something
o you?"

Damn the man! He was going to ask for money, after all.

"It would."

"How much money would it be worth?"

"A considerable sum."

"I will see what I can do."

"You cannot tell me now?" snapped Gervase, impatiently. "Why can't you?"

"Give me your card and your direction. I shall make inquiries, and let you know what I find," he said smoothly, taking his leave. He left at once, chuckling and singing to himself, happy for the first time since he had lost five hundred pounds at Heathdown. It was true! It had to be true! Sarratt's little serving-wench was a light-skirt—or a thief—perhaps both!

The lad would pay handsomely to find her, or perhaps she would pay handsomely not to be found. It all depended on what objects she had taken, or what property she held. Yes, life could change quite quickly, just like one's luck at cards.

Chapter 23

On the morning of the dinner party which would be
the first formal social encounter between the Wellesford
and Rutherfurd families, the dowager had received the
reply to her hastily written letter of inquiry. The swift
response came in the form of a visit from her dear old
friend the Countess of Tremont, a woman who was
delightfully knowledgeable about genealogy and the peer-
age, ancient heraldic symbols, and suchlike. The countess,
a large, stately woman of uncertain age, arrived with her
personal footman, who bore with him three large, leather-
bound books.

Her footman behind her, she was shown up to the
dowager's sitting-room, where the two women embraced
one another fondly.

"I came as soon as I could after I got your note. You
must explain this mystery to me, and I shall explain to
you what I have discovered."

"I am afraid that, at this point at least, the matter is

rather delicate," said the dowager, referring to the pres‐
ence of the footman.

"Indeed so," replied the countess. "John, you ma
leave the books on that table, and kindly wait for m
downstairs in the hall."

Once her footman had withdrawn, the countess move
over to a chair quite close to her friend.

"Now," she announced, "tell me what this is a
about!"

The Dowager Duchess of Sarratt went to her desk
unlocked a drawer, and brought out the sketch she ha
made of the ruby ring.

"This ring was found in this house yesterday. I hel
it myself: it was made of fine gold, with a very excellen
ruby set in the center. What I wish to know is, to whic
great family does the ring belong? Can you determin
that from looking at its crest?"

"To be sure, I can. It is only a matter of time, my dea
May I ask how this ring was 'found,' as you put it, i
your house?"

"Diana discovered it in the possession of her abigail.'

"Good God! Her girl will hang for it!" cried the Count
ess of Tremont.

"That is very much what I am afraid of."

"Very well. Let us begin to look at once. We mus
hope that it turns out to belong to someone with whor
one of us is acquainted, so that we can arrange to retur
the ring privately to its real owner, make amends, an
hush the whole thing up. One really does *not* wish t
involve oneself in scandal."

Trying to forget the difficulties attached to having he
father's ring found in her possession, wanting to immers
herself in her work, Lady Mary had taken great pains a

during the day over the dressing of her mistress, Diana Leigh. She had wound Miss Diana's hair up in curls early on, and had encouraged her to rest the whole day before, drinking chamomile tea and bathing her eyes in cool water.

Miss Diana made no further reference to the fabulous ring, for which Lady Mary was immensely grateful. It was bad enough that she was going to have to find a way of explaining the thing to the Duchess of Sarratt—if she could not come up with some plausible excuse, she would be out on the street, in the middle of London, with nowhere to go.

The Duke of Sarratt, following Lord Weymouth's advice, had gone out of his way to avoid any further contact with the girl Mary, lest her sheer presence serve to weaken his resolve. After he returned from Weymouth's lodgings, he had secreted himself in his library, resigned to his fate and depressed by it. He felt sure she would know he was deliberately avoiding her.

Foremost on his mind, of course, was the matter of tonight's dinner party for Lady Adelaide and her family, which would be the first formal signal to the ton of his marital intentions.

Though Mary was the one he would have wished for, coming to know her as perfectly as he knew his own reflection, he must, in good conscience, marry Adelaide. No matter that the Duke of Argyll had married the Gunning girl—misalliances such as that were, just as Weymouth had said, a thing of the past.

Upon reflection, he had come to understand Weymouth's point of view, and to make it his own. Truly, his dear mother would never forgive him, nor, indeed, could he ever forgive himself for disgracing his family's good name in a low marriage. Weymouth had been right; indeed in his own heart, the duke had always known the truth.

Having conceded that point, there was another thing that had begun to weigh on his mind: could he, in good conscience, attempt to persuade the girl to change her mind, and become his mistress? If he applied pressure, would she relent? He wanted her, but he would have given anything not to have to make the choice of giving her up forever, or, by keeping her, deprive Mary of her good character. On the other hand, was he prepared to resign himself to her loss? He was not.

Since he had spoken to Weymouth, the duke had assiduously avoided his mother's quarters, he had avoided Diana's sitting-room; he had kept himself away from any area of the house in which he might inadvertently come across Mary. He had made a decision, a good one, a proper one, the right one, and he would not be diverted from it.

He immured himself in his books and his records of business, waiting for the time when he must dress for dinner.

After several hours' work, the two ladies were triumphant.

"This is it!" announced the Countess of Tremont. "The ring most definitely bears the coat of arms of the Earl of Hamilton."

"I can't recall who is the earl these days. I don't believe I've seen the family in town for many years, do you?"

"There was one who died in a carriage accident, wasn't there?"

"I believe so. Something about breaking down on the highway, in a snowstorm. The poor man was injured, and froze to death."

"Terrible."

"Who was his heir? Do you recall?"

"I do not, but I think their house is still kept in town, on Belgrave Square."

"That's where I shall try to make contact with them, then. Today, I shall send Thomas, along with this drawing I made of the ring, over to Hamilton House. I will tell the family that I have discovered the whereabouts of the ring, and then together we'll try to settle this unfortunate matter in a very discreet way."

"Let me know how it turns out, my dear. Thank you so much for letting me assist you in your little project. So mysterious! It was most exciting!"

"I only wish you could stay around to watch this Mary's face when I inform her that I know all about where she got her ring."

Thomas, bearing her grace's packet, was sent to an address where he had never before been: Hamilton House in Belgrave Square. The Hamilton House porter informed Thomas that the current owner's name was Sir Barton Ayleston, and that Sir Barton was expected to arrive from out of town momentarily. He was also informed that Mr. Gervase Ayleston, Sir Barton's nephew, was in residence as well, but that Mr. Ayleston had just gone out on urgent business. Would Thomas care to wait?

It was four o'clock before Thomas returned, carrying with him a respectful letter for the Dowager Duchess of Sarratt from Sir Barton Ayleston of Hamilton House, Belgrave Square. It thanked her grace for the trouble she had taken to locate him; he assured her that the ring in question was a missing heirloom belonging to the family of the Earl of Hamilton, for whom he was executor. If it would be convenient for her grace, Sir Barton and his nephew Gervase wished to **call tomorrow** morning to call at Sarratt House, in order to **recover the** item as quickly as possible.

The duchess had been wondering whether she ought to confront Mary immediately with her intelligence as to the rightful ownership of the ring she had so obviously stolen. Now, she decided it would be best to wait until morning.

Diana, after all, still had to be dressed, and the dear girl would undoubtedly be upset when she learned that her maid had been confirmed to be a thief. If Diana became upset, she would undoubtedly cry, and ruin her looks.

The matter could wait until morning.

When the time for dinner arrived, Diana was the tangle of nerves she had always been, but with Mary there to cosset her and cajole her, and restore her confidence in herself, she emerged from her room triumphant, looking as pretty as she ever had, and feeling confident she was in good looks for the Earl of Weymouth.

Mary had persuaded Diana to wear one of her finest new gowns, of blue, trimmed with lace at the bosom and flounce. Her hair was piled atop her head, with a filet of blue satin threaded through it. She wore a set of pearls with matching pearl earrings. All in all, the effect was enchanting.

When she came down to stand next to her guardian and his mother at the top of the staircase, to welcome their guests, Diana looked very much the thing.

The duke, seeing the transformation in his ward that undoubtedly was due to Mary's good influence, was both proud of Diana and grateful to Mary. Those warm feelings toward Mary, however, were not going to deter him from his resolve to do the right thing by his family tonight.

Many of the servants, including Lady Mary, had settled themselves variously on the second floor landing, so as to catch a glimpse through the banisters of the elegant proceedings. Even Mrs. Brindle, who really shouldn't have been tempted to look, thought that his grace was looking particularly handsome in a snow-white waistcoat, knee breeches, and a black coat cut without an inch to spare, white stockings and black slippers.

Everyone knew (since Boswell repeated the fact endlessly) that his grace's coats were cut by the inimitable Weston; however the beautiful fit across his chest and shoulders, entirely free of padding, was evidence of the time he had spent at Gentleman Jackson's. His grace's cravat was done in a high fall of his own invention that none other could duplicate, though many had tried.

Lord and Lady Rutherfurd came with two of their three grown children, Lady Adelaide Henchart and the Hon. Roger Henchart; supporting the duke was his friend, Lord Weymouth, looking very gay.

The dowager duchess was dressed in a mauve gown, with handmade lace at the throat and hem, crowned with a diamond tiara; Lady Rutherfurd was in green, wearing a matching turban.

Lady Adelaide Henchart was wearing a rose-colored gown, rather excessively ornamented. As soon as she was greeted by the duke, she began to cling to him. She followed him around from room to room like a puppy, hanging on the duke's every word, laughing in what she must have thought an attractive manner, and poking his arm for emphasis every now and then. It occurred to the dowager that Lady Adelaide was beginning to look a tad desperate.

Once the guests were all assembled, Lady Rutherfurd

went in on the duke's arm, and the dowager on the arm of the earl of Rutherfurd. Lord Rutherfurd, who had a strong cold, kept blowing his nose, and looked as though he wished himself elsewhere.

Lord Weymouth, dressed excellently in a black coat by Scott, escorted Lady Adelaide Henchart to the table, while the Hon. Diana Leigh went in on the arm of the Hon. Roger, all in strict order of precedence.

The table had been set with the best china and napery; a forest of candles sparkled on the walls and from above. The silver epergne that caused the housemaids so much grief to polish sparkled in the center, looking very grand.

Guests were seated, and service began: dishes in silver-topped servers that had been buffed to a high gloss were brought in and laid out, holding various culinary delights, which were the result of the combined hard labor of all the kitchen staff, from Cook all the way to Jane Marshman, the scullery maid who had peeled the potatoes and plucked the fowl.

Conversation commenced with each person speaking to the guest on his right. Roger had been reminded by his ever-alert mama that Diana was a considerable heiress; seated next to her at the table, he spent his time trying his best to flatter her and flirt with her. Diana, however, had eyes only for Lord Weymouth, while, to her dismay, a famished Lord Weymouth had eyes for naught but his turbot.

Lady Mary spent most of dinnertime upstairs in Miss Diana's chamber, restoring it to order after the usual scramble to dress her mistress. There was to be musical entertainment after dinner, and she had been told by Mrs. Brindle that, once her work was finished, she could listen from a draped alcove to the side of the music room.

By the time Mary had time to come downstairs, dinner was over, the ladies had withdrawn, and then returned. Diana was at the pianoforte playing and singing, and Lord Weymouth, attentive once more, was turning the pages for her.

Watching her, Mary was very proud of the changes she had helped Diana make; when the girl's appearance improved to the point where she was complimented on it, she had relaxed, and her natural charm had come to the fore. Mary wondered how long it would be before Weymouth paid a formal visit to the duke, asking for his ward's hand in marriage.

So rapt was Lady Mary in listening to the music, and speculating on the progress of Diana Leigh's romance, that she did not hear the duke and Lady Adelaide approaching the quiet corner of the room where she was listening.

The duke and Lady Adelaide had seated themselves next to one another on a loveseat within earshot of her before she realized they were there. For a moment, she was paralyzed: would it be more embarrassing now to make her escape and leave? or would it be worse to stay?

When his grace took Lady Adelaide's hand in his, Lady Mary realized she should have left, at all costs. She realized, with horror, what his grace was up to.

"Adelaide, I have known you all of my life," his familiar, deep voice was saying. "Our families are well-known to each other; connexions between them have been the exception rather than the rule for many centuries. I have always had a profound respect for you and for your family."

"I have felt that, Duke."

"There comes a time in a man's life—" his grace stopped here, the words he did not at all wish to say were catching in his throat.

He tried again, saying, "There comes a time in a man's life when he thinks about continuing his lineage, and doing so, he looks to find a suitable life-partner."

Lady Adelaide felt a surge of joy pass through her being such as she had never known before. At last! Coming up to scratch at last!

She squeezed his grace's hand tightly; with some difficulty, the duke was able not to withdraw it.

"Persons such as ourselves, Adelaide, are not bound by the—how shall I say?—more romantic dispositions typical of the lower classes."

Lady Mary Hamilton, listening to this rubbish, was dying a thousand deaths behind the curtain. It was bad enough to be trapped there, but did she really have to withstand a repetition of this man's class prejudice? Was she really going to have to endure overhearing the man she undoubtedly loved proposing marriage to another woman?

"She who would fulfill the position of Duchess of Sarratt must have many good qualities: being of excellent family, having been properly brought up, and willing to attend to the many details necessary in the wife of a peer."

The Sarratt jewels! Lady Adelaide said to herself. *I will be wearing the Sarratt jewels! Nobody will have such things as I! I will give the most famous parties, I will have as many carriages as I wish, I will be the toast of London!* Her heart surged with a happiness she had never before known.

"Expressing, if I may," said the duke, "my high regard for your personal qualities, I must ask you, Lady Adelaide, will you do me the honor—"

Unable to contain herself, unable to endure this scene a moment longer, Lady Mary, her face bright red, threw aside the draperies, saying, with as much dignity as she

ıld muster," I do beg your pardon, your grace, Lady
elaide. I am rather *de trop."*

Lady Mary bolted toward the door, swiftly exiting the
ɔm as Lady Adelaide and the duke jumped to their feet.

''It's that maid of yours again!" shrieked Lady Ade-
ɟe, drawing the attention of everyone in the musicroom,
ɫ briefly interrupting the performance of Diana Leigh,
ɔ had been sweetly singing some country airs.

The duke, completely mortified, walked over to the
ɩnoforte and began to discuss some obscure musical
ɔstions with his ward and his friend Lord Weymouth,
t as if nothing had been amiss.

The Hon. Roger Henchart, from a vantage point near
ɩ window, had seen the disturbance with interest; he
ɔndered what was going on between his sister, the duke,
ɫ the abigail, and how he might best be able to capitalize
ɔn it. Deep as he was in the River Tick, he needed to
n events to his own advantage.

Henchart left the music room by a side door, and then
ɭbled back down the hall, trying to find the room where
ɩ girl had fled.

Lady Mary went straight into the formal library, a little-
ɛd room which she knew to be empty and which had
ᴠays been one of the best places in the house to enjoy
ɩttle solitude. She opened the door, ran in, and threw
ʳself on a chair, beginning to weep bitterly.

She felt it was the end of everything.

When she thought of the words that the duke had spoken
her in the park, offering her his friendship, she felt
ɭrayed and ashamed. What had happened since then?
ɩce their encounter in the park, the Duke of Sarratt had
ɩe out of his way to avoid being in her presence.

The duke's offering of his friendship was just the same
that offered by Roger Henchart: they both were looking
ɟet me up as their mistress, the duke for the second time.

Obviously, he had intended all along to marry Henchar, sister, a girl of good family for whom he has neither lo, nor respect. I hate the duke. I hate Henchart. I hate the, all!

Sarratt spoke kindly words to me, but only to make n, trust him again. He had no personal feelings of friendsh, toward me—he had only dishonorable intentions cloak, in honeyed words.

This whole affair has ended in complete disaster. T, duke thinks me beneath his notice, fit for a slip on t, shoulder and nothing more.

She took her father's ring from around her neck a, stared at it, dolefully.

The duchess thinks me a thief because I have my de, father's ring in my possession. I cannot reveal the tru, or risk exposure, lest I risk becoming Lady Mary Aylesto, and spending the rest of my life with that evil man.

I shall leave here at first light. I wish I were dead.

"I wish I were dead," she whispered aloud.

"Pray, do not be so dramatic, Mary," said the voi, of Roger Henchart. "Do not despair. I feel sure I c, contribute to your well-being, if we can but make a mut, ally agreeable arrangement."

Mary got up at once, shocked, but Roger clapped o, hand on her mouth, and put one hand around her wai, pulling her tightly to him.

"Don't scream, pretty Mary. I know now who you ar, and what you are. Promise you won't scream and I'll, go."

Mary nodded agreement, tears in her eyes.

"What's that in your hand?" he demanded.

"Nothing."

"Give it me," said Roger, wrenching the ruby ring c, of her hand. "Well, well, my girl: so *this* is what th,

low was talking about. Tell me, Mary, how came you
ross such a pretty little trinket?"

"It's mine. Give it back to me," she said, trying to
atch it back from him.

"I think I will not give it back. I think that you must
ve done something *very* naughty, my dear, to be in
ssession of a ring so magnificent as this one. Two
ssibilities occur to me: either you stole it, or it was a
t to you from a wealthy lover. Which is the case?"

"Neither. Give it back," she said in a tone of warning,
ndering if she could find an object with which to strike
n.

"By the way, my dear, speaking of wealthy lovers, did
ell you that I came across a certain gentleman from the
rth of England who had come to London apparently
r the sole purpose of making inquiries about you?"

Mary's eyes went wide with shock and fear. Sir Barton?
rvase?

"Yes, I felt sure you would be interested. The gentle-
an was even carrying around a painted miniature of
u, showing it all around, here and there and everywhere,
d asking whether or not people knew you. The picture
s a very fair likeness of you: that's what made you
her easy to recognize.

"Don't worry, my child," he said in a purring voice.
was very discreet. I did not precisely admit that I knew
u, although I believe the man gained the impression
at I did, and now knows that you are to be found some-
ere in London.

"Now, let me see if I can recall his name—Allston, was
Ilsington? I have it—the fellow's name was Ayleston,
rvase Ayleston—of Danby Court, I think it was, in
mberland. Do you know him, my dear?"

Lady Mary let out an audible gasp.

Hearing this, the Hon. Roger Henchart's smile broad‐ ened considerably.

"Don't despair, Mary. No doubt it will take some littl‐ time for Mr. Ayleston to discover your *exact* where‐ abouts—unless I should decide to reveal them to him— so perhaps, under the circumstances, we could discus‐ the terms for my continued silence."

"What terms?" whispered Lady Mary.

"Or, if you feel yourself reluctant to come to term‐ with me, perhaps I really ought to be discussing with *hi‐* my terms for handing you over to him."

"Don't turn me over to him," she said desperately. ‐ beg you, do not do that."

"But you must appreciate my curiosity about the enti‐ situation. Did he give you that ruby ring in a moment ‐ passion, which he now regrets? Or did you merely ste‐ the ring from him? I wish to know with whom I a‐ dealing, you see.

"If you are a thief, the prospect of being caught is mo‐ distasteful, particularly when theft is a hanging offense. ‐ you are a runaway mistress who had been handsome‐ rewarded for your favors, you must have had good reaso‐ to run away."

Lady Mary, frozen, made no reply.

"It is also logical to suggest you must be capable ‐ performing favors extremely well, if I may be so bold ‐ to mention it."

Lady Mary's cheeks began to burn with humiliatio‐ but what was she supposed to do? If she crossed him, ‐ would set the Aylestons on her in a minute. Roger Henc‐ art took her silence as consent.

"It is those favors, you must appreciate, which are ‐ most interest to me. That being the case, I feel sure th‐ you will decide in favor of my proposal: come and li‐ under my protection. I will set you up in town. In tim‐

am sure you will learn to be grateful to me. You shall,
f course, never steal from me, nor are you to expect
xtravagant gifts. I will maintain you, and visit you as
nd when I wish, and in return, I shall keep our little
ecret.

"Let us seal our bargain with a kiss—"

The Hon. Roger pulled Mary roughly to him; she strug-
led to free herself, but he was very strong.

"Our arrangement is all settled, then?"

"Yes! But I must have the ring back!"

Chapter 24

The Duke of Sarratt entered the formal library just in
ne to overhear this last exchange. He had come in search
' Mary, shaken to the core by what had happened in the
usic room. Sudden realization of the truth had come
)on him, and he had just made the hardest decision of
s life: he had realized what utter disaster would occur
he married Lady Adelaide Henchart. He would not offer
r her, and if her family wished to sue him for breach
promise, they could do so, with his blessing. He would
mply buy them off.

The duke had come to the library with a heart full of
ve and hope, now fully prepared to ask Mary Simpson,
s own housemaid, to become her grace Mary, Duchess
Sarratt.

As to the reactions of family, friends, and society: he
ould let the chips fall where they may.

However, when Sarratt entered the room, he beheld
e sight of his beloved Mary in the full embrace of Roger

Henchart, and did not know which emotion had take
more possession of him: jealousy or anger.

He strode over to the couple, and pushed Roger roughl
away.

"Roger, you will leave this house directly."

"Why, Sarratt! You are unnecessarily alarmed. Wh
harm is there in stealing a kiss from your pretty littl
maid?"

"Do your procuring in Drury Lane, not in my house.

"Oh, very well. But I don't see what harm there ca
be in stealing a kiss from a pretty thief. Did you kno
that your little maid here is a thief, Sarratt? Have yo
seen this?" said he, maliciously, holding up the magnif
cent ring.

The duke's heart, already shaken by finding the woma
he loved in a compromising position with a rake of th
first order, sank even lower as he examined the ruby rin
Roger Henchart was holding up to the light.

"That ring is mine, sir," said Lady Mary desperatel

"Give the girl back the ring, Roger," said the duk
wearily. "Try another scheme to settle your debts."

"I can't see why you're being so old-fashioned,
replied Henchart, annoyed.

"Leave my house. Now."

"Beware of that girl, Sarratt. There's more to her tha
first appears," said the Hon. Roger, giving the ring to th
duke, and leaving the room.

The duke, whose face had gone perfectly whit
motioned a mortified, speechless Mary to a seat, for h
was not finished with her, not at all.

He inspected the ring with great care. It was no pas
copy, as he had hoped it might be. No, it was the re
thing: a priceless pigeon's-blood red ruby, mounted on
solid gold base fashioned in the shape of a family cres

was not merely a ring belonging to a gentleman, but a
ng belonging to a nobleman.

For the duke, the ring was proof positive. His precious
Iary, who had preyed on his mind for so long, had been
omeone's ladybird already, and that ring had been reward
or her services.

"Doxy," he said to her bitterly, shaking his head. "I
ad not thought it of you."

He fairly threw the ring at her.

"You deceived me all too well, Mary. You deceived
ly staff. You deceived my ward. You deceived my own
lother with that fairy story about the late deacon, your
ather who taught you to read, and his houseful of children.
Vhat utter nonsense you regaled us with.

"Lady Adelaide warned me against you, but I did not
sten. Weymouth warned me against you, but I would
ot listen to him, blinded by my feelings for you. Everyone
old me that a girl with looks like yours has no place in
ervice, that sooner or later you would cause trouble. So
t has turned out. I thought that you were different, I
lought you kind and gentle, but you are not.

"I came here to this room, prepared to offer for your
and in marriage. I was prepared to make a fool of Lady
delaide, to make a fool of myself, and to diminish forever
ly family's good name in the eyes of society, and all
ecause I was in love with you.

"What is my reward? Learning my love's true nature.
earning that you, Mary, are a thief, and a woman of
asy virtue. Learning that you are deceitful; learning that
ou are, as Adelaide warned me long ago, no better than
ou should be. You are ignorant, like the rest of your
ind, and you are driven by greed and by lust, and not
y the higher instincts.

"Go ahead—become Henchart's mistress if you

wish—but not while you are living under my roof, and not while you are attending my innocent ward.

"Please forgive me that, having learned your true nature, I find myself unable to offer for your hand."

He turned away from her; she could see that he was shaking with anger. Listening to his words, she had begun to tremble with feeling herself.

"Twice you have wronged me, Duke, through your blindness and your prejudice. You believe only the evidence of your eyes, but you deny the evidence of your heart. The visible evidence in this case is misleading; I tell you that you are wrong, utterly wrong, about my circumstances. You believe the word of Roger Henchart because he is of your own class, and you disbelieve me because you believe me to be lowly.

"Indeed, many another man would have at least *inquired* of me what had happened here tonight, and ask why I carry this ring upon my person; another man would at least have had the good grace to ask me to reveal my side of the story.

"You did not even ask me to tell my tale. You did not for the same reason you wronged me before: sheer prejudice.

"In your heart, you must know I am innocent—indeed in your heart, you must feel my innocence, but because your intellect informs you that I am low born, you think the worst of me, and cast me aside.

"I feel sorry for you, Duke. I feel sorry for anyone who is so blind and so unjust and so unfair. I am not what you think I am. I am what your heart felt all along; much good may it do you."

His grace of Sarratt, still trembling with rage, paced around the library in an attempt to maintain control over himself. He would not allow himself to look at the beauti-

l, scheming creature who still sat, stiffly, on the edge
f a gilded seat.

At last the duke felt master of himself to reply, carefully,
I know not who you may be, ma'am, or what you truly
e, but one thing is sure: you are certainly not the person
ou represented yourself to be when you came into service
this house. Thus, at the very least, I may honestly call
ou a liar."

"Stop!" she cried. "I have done with you. I would
corn to be your wife. I will listen to your insults no
onger. I am leaving."

"As you wish, Mary," he said coldly.

Chapter 25

Mary, deep in tears, flew out of the library, and ran up
two flights of stairs to her little closet. She shut the door
hard, and threw herself down on her pallet, weeping
uncontrollably. She pushed her head into her pillow to
smother the sobs, but she knew she could be heard in
Diana's room. It did not matter, anyhow. Nothing mattered
anymore.

The things he had said to her! The things he had thought
about her! It was too much to bear.

Why, why had she not remained downstairs, dusting
and polishing? Why had she given in to laziness and to
pride, and allowed herself to come upstairs into the world
of the quality? It had only brought her suffering, and now,
the mistakes she had made there would cost her dearly.

She felt the four walls of the world inexorably closing
in on her.

There was the matter of the ring. She should never
have worn it at all: it was just too dangerous. Now, at
Garratt House, it seemed that everyone knew all about

the ring: Diana, the dowager, the duke. That miscalcula‐
tion was going to cost her, who knew how much?

Roger Henchart knew all about the ring, too, and ha
it not been for the duke's intervention, he would hav
blackmailed her.

Then, thanks to Roger Henchart, she had learned abo
the Aylestons.

Now they knew she was in London; they were in Lon
don to track her down, and Henchart had obviously hinte
to them that he knew where she was. It was only a matt
of time before they discovered the range of Henchart
acquaintances: the trail from Henchart to Lady Adelaid
to the duke to herself was a straight line.

Sarratt House was no longer a place of refuge, it wa
a trap.

The duke was upstairs in his personal library the ne
morning when Weymouth called. Lord Weymout
appeared to be in the highest of spirits, a circumstanc
which only underscored the poor spirits of his frien
Boswell, the duke's valet, could attest to the fact that h
grace had slept not a wink all night. He had tossed an
turned on his mattress; gotten up and paced around f
some time, tried to sleep, paced, and lay in bed agai
contemplating the ceiling and the bleakness of his futur
life.

He could not believe that, after so many years, of a
women, his heart had been captured by a beautiful lia
but there it was. He thought of her being taken away b
the authorities; he thought of her being transported
Australia; he thought of her being hung by the neck
a gibbet until dead, all with some satisfaction.

When he thought of how angry he was with her,

genuinely wished her dead; in more rational moods, he wondered if he should not try to protect her from the consequences of her actions.

It was this mood that Lord Weymouth interrupted; his mood bright and cheerful, and, to the duke, unbearable.

"Charles! You're not lookin' well! What's wrong?"

"Nothing."

"Oh, well. That's a shame. At all events, Sarratt, there's something I'd like to ask. Here's the thing: Diana."

"What about her?" snapped the duke.

"Well, the thing is . . . spent a lot of time with the girl these past weeks. Got to know her. Like her."

"Yes?" he asked suspiciously

"Fell in love with her. Want to marry her. With your consent, of course. Came to ask for it."

"Marry her? You?" asked the duke.

Lord Weymouth looked nonplussed.

"It ain't all that strange. I know I've been a bachelor, and no one thought I was in the line for marriage. Didn't think so myself. One day it just happened."

"I see," said the duke gloomily. "It just happened. Like falling down the stairs."

"Not so bad as that. Thing is, Charles, may I? I'll be a good husband to her."

"She's too young to marry. She's hardly out."

"Says she'll have me."

The duke exploded.

"She's too young, and you're too old! What do you know about women and their ways, James? What if she's not what you think she is?"

"What else would she be, man?" said the earl, polishing his quizzing-glass with his handkerchief.

"She might well be someone you had no idea of! No, you can't marry now. I won't allow it."

"I've never seen you in such a state, Sarratt. What's the matter with you?"

"Nothing!" he shouted. "Nothing!"

The next morning, Lady Mary had packed all her possessions into her leather case, and was all ready to go. She had only to decide how to do it. Over the night, she had come to understand that her situation was much more serious than she had at first supposed.

To wait at Sarratt House for a chaperone to come to her was really not possible. They were ready to call for the authorities as it was. The thought of her leaving or her own, making her way about London as a lone female, one who did not know the city, one who had no friends, was daunting, and Lady Mary Hamilton was very much afraid.

One of the maids came to her, and told her that she had been relieved of her morning duties with Miss Diana, but was to go to the dowager's sittingroom at once and wait for her. Not knowing what else to do, she went, and she waited for the duchess to speak with her.

Sir Barton Ayleston and his nephew Gervase called at Sarratt House bright and early that morning. They showed the letter they had received from her grace, and, on that basis, the hall porter had them shown up to the main parlor. Her grace, they said, was still breakfasting, but their names would be taken in to her once she was done.

Almost on impulse, Sir Barton asked whether his grace the duke was at home. Thomas, the footman who had shown them to the parlor, said that he would inquire. Sir Barton asked that the letter and sketch he had received from the dowager duchess be shown to the duke, in order

) authenticate their visit, and Thomas bowed and took
1em up. In addition, they asked that the duke be told
1eir visit involved an urgent search for a missing heirloom
ng.

Receiving this message, anxious that his family's name
e attached to no scandal, the duke had them shown to
is sitting-room at once.

The duke gave them back the letter, saying, "This
cetch appears to have been done by my mother. Could
ou tell me, how is she involved in this?"

"I do not precisely know. I was quite surprised, yester-
ay, when we received it, and that is the reason we came.
Ve are looking for a ruby ring that is part of a priceless
ollection of jewels belonging to the family of the late
arl of Hamilton."

"We believe your mother must have knowledge of its
·hereabouts."

"I see."

"There is a girl involved, as well."

"What girl?"

"There was a girl who once lived at Danby Court. Very
nusual-looking—you would remember her instantly, had
ou ever seen her."

"Would I?" asked the duke noncommittally.

"Raven-black hair, violet eyes, very fair skin. A dia-
10nd of the first water—a woman impossible to forget.
Ve believe she is connected to the disappearance of the
ng. Would your grace have seen such a girl, by any
1ance?"

It was time to throw the girl to the wolves, the duke
1ld himself. It was, after all, only what she deserved.

"Yes. I have. As it happens, there is such a girl in this
ery household."

"May we . . . speak with her, your grace? Not wishing
• raise any scandal, may we speak with her privately?"

"Yes, of course."

He rang for his man, and asked that Mary be broug at once to his sitting-room.

Not waiting for her to come, not wanting to see th face of the deceiver, the duke bowed himself out befo she came, saying graciously, "Gentlemen, I will lea you to your business, then."

Chapter 26

"Thank you, my child, for trusting me with your story," said the dowager to Lady Mary Hamilton, pressing her hand warmly. "I promise you that I shall find a safe place for you to stay until you come of age. No one will harm you. No one will force you to do anything you do not wish."

"Thank you, your grace, for believing me."

"The story you told me, unusual though it was, was perhaps the only one that could explain everything that has happened, and everything that you are. I am not surprised to learn that you are the daughter of a peer; I am happy for you.

"I am only sorry that you have had so many difficulties in your life, ones which you have had to face without the support of your family. That is over now."

"I was so frightened to tell you—but I had no one else to turn to. Your son, the duke, was so angry with me last night."

"He did not know the truth, did he?"

"No. I was angry with him, as well. I did not tell him who I was."

"You must forgive him."

At this point, Thomas scratched on the door.

"Pardon me, your grace: I was told that Mary is with you."

"She is."

"His grace is wishful that she come straightaway to his sitting-room."

Lady Mary looked questioningly at the dowager.

"Go ahead now and see him. There's nothing to be afraid of. Tell him the truth this time, won't you? Tell him precisely who and what you are."

"Yes, ma'am. I will. Thank you again for all your kindness to me."

Lady Mary left the duchess's suite with trepidation. She was reluctant, after all this time, to reveal her true identity to the duke. She knew the duchess wished her not to hold a grudge against him, but she could not help herself: his words had been so hurtful.

She knew she had to face him, sooner or later. How bad could it be? What could he do to her, after all, that he had not already done? Could he say anything more awful than he had already?

She opened the door to his grace's own sitting-room and she was confronted with a scene from a deadly nightmare.

On two gilt chairs were sitting Sir Barton Ayleston and his nephew Gervase, a look of triumph on their faces.

His grace the Duke of Sarratt was nowhere to be seen.

Lady Mary Hamilton gave a small, helpless cry, and then dropped to the floor, unconscious.

Gervase ran over to her crumpled form, lifted her up

and put her on a couch. He chafed her hands, a delighted smile upon his face.

"There, there. It's all right. You're in good hands again, Lady Mary."

Lady Mary came to and began to weep.

"You ran us a good fight, Lady Mary. I congratulate you. But it's all over now, and you've come back to us."

Rising to her feet, Lady Mary angrily responded, "No, I have not come back to you. You surprised me. I have friends in this house. The dowager duchess is my friend. She will not permit you to take me away, do you hear? Your scheme is over. It has ended. It has failed. I do not know why his grace consented to see you, or why you may be running tame around his house, but it does not matter."

"Lady Mary, you will be coming with us."

"I will not. I refuse to go with you. Good-day, gentlemen," she said, and she turned to leave. Sir Barton grabbed her wrist, and held it roughly.

"Let go of me at once, or I shall scream for help."

"There are things you need to know, Lady Mary. I do not think you have considered the seriousness of your situation."

"I am among friends. I am safe. You cannot harm me anymore."

"Not wanting to contradict you, Lady Mary, I'm afraid we can harm you very much, and very easily. In point of fact, it is you who have harmed yourself: we are the only instruments who can save your reputation."

"My reputation?"

"Yes. You appear not to have considered that, due to the eccentricities of your own actions, you can now never marry anyone except Gervase."

"I'd kill myself before I'd marry Gervase."

"No, you wouldn't. You'll come with us. Now."

"Don't be ridiculous."

"Come, come, Lady Mary. The ton is a small and very particular world; the only way to make an eligible marriage is to have an entree to polite society, something that is not given lightly. Think of the patronesses at Almack's: would the haughty Mrs. Drummond-Burrell issue vouchers to a girl who has been posing as a housemaid? Never in this world."

She was afraid she was going to faint again, and sank into a seat, placing her head in her hands.

"Would Maria Sefton," said Sir Barton, "willingly give vouchers to a girl who has spent the night unchaperoned in the company of a man? Never."

"No one knows of that!" she cried, looking up at him with alarm.

"Yes, they do, your ladyship. Everyone in town knows of it. What do you think we have been doing all this time, while searching for you? Did you think we did not put it about that you had eloped with Gervase? Of course we did."

"We said that it was all your idea, too," added Gervase gleefully. "We spread around that you are a wild, uncontrollable, care-for-nothing hoyden. Not just in Cumberland: we have spread the tale all around London."

"Everyone knows the tale of Lady Mary Hamilton by now. Other than Gervase, no one else will ever want you. No one else will ever marry you."

Recognizing the truth of this, Lady Mary began to feel physically ill.

No one else will marry you.

Suddenly the words sank into her consciousness and she realized what they meant. In that moment, she admitted to herself that she was deeply in love with the Duke of Sarratt, and that she had loved him from the first.

In that moment she realized that Sir Barton and Gervase

were perfectly correct: the duke, like the rest of the peers and gentlemen of the ton, would never marry her. No matter that he would learn the details of her gentle birth, he would never have her, for her good name had been sullied beyond repair.

Would a man with such deep family pride allow himself to be made the laughing-stock of London? Would such a man think to wed a girl whose name was synonymous with scandal?

Which did she prefer? Scandal and abject public humiliation? Rejection by the man she loved? Marriage to Gervase Ayleston?

What difference did it make?

She was as good as dead already.

Unable to deal with the painful reality of her situation, she went pale ashen-white, and lost consciousness once again, falling back onto the satin chair.

Sir Barton quickly signaled to Gervase, and then it was all over in a matter of moments.

With no servant in attendance senior enough to be willing to call the behavior of gentlemen into question, Gervase had only to take Lady Mary Hamilton's small, limp form into his arms, and carry her swiftly down the long marble staircase and out the front door, which he did in an instant.

Sir Barton brusquely informed the porter that a girl of their acquaintance had fallen desperately ill, that there was not a moment to lose, and even himself opened the carriage door.

Gervase placed Lady Mary on the back seat of their carriage, the one emblazoned with the Hamilton crest, just as it was on the earl's ring. He told the coachman to spring the horses, and Lady Mary Hamilton, still unconscious, was taken away from Sarratt House.

Chapter 27

Susan Bowker had been asked to perform a task she found demeaning: cleaning out the tiny closet where Mary Simpson used to sleep. As Mrs. Brindle had specifically commissioned her to do so, she was unable to refuse. Still, it didn't sit well with her.

As she was dusting, she came across Mary's leather box, which had always interested her. Angry, she looked to see if anyone was around. Thinking herself safe, she began to rifle through it. It took her few moments to reach the bottom, where her fingers closed around a heavy velvet bag. She drew it out of the box and opened it.

The bag was full of jewels. Mary was a thief!

For a moment, Susan was of two minds as to what to do: if she nicked the stuff herself, Mary most likely wouldn't do a thing about it. How would she be able to complain of missing things she shouldn't have had in the first place? Susan would become richer than her wildest dreams. She could become a fine lady, and wear silk and drink wine and eat cakes.

Susan indulged this daydream for a few moments, and then pulled out of it. She'd better tell someone, or maybe she'd get hanged instead of Mary, who so richly deserved it. Should she tell Mrs. Brindle? Or Mr. Buckley? Perhaps she should go straight to the duke?

She decided on the latter strategy. Perhaps she could raise her status in the household if she were thought to be an honest girl.

She looked to see if the duke was in his sitting-room, but there were only two gentlemen talking to Mary. That was odd.

She went upstairs to his grace's private bookroom, and peering through a crack in the door, found him, sitting in his favorite chair, scowling.

It hardly seemed like his grace was in a mood to receive more bad news, but Susan knew she certainly couldn't keep the jewels on her own person a minute longer, and thought she'd be better off dealing with the duke than with the steward. She scratched on the door and went in.

"Your grace?" she ventured timidly.

"What is it?" he snapped.

"Meanin' no harm, your grace, I was cleanin' around Miss Diana's room, in the place where that Mary stays, and I bumped her case, not meanin' to, and her case fell open and then I found these."

She handed the black velvet bag to him.

The duke, staring at the bag in disbelief, opened it and brought out a fabulous emerald necklace.

"This was in Mary's case, you say?"

"Yes, yer grace. I was afraid when I saw it, so I thought to bring it straight to you, beggin' yer pardon."

"You did just right. Susan, isn't it? You did very well indeed, Susan. Very good judgment in coming to me. I'll take care of this; you may go."

The duke knows my name! Very pleased with herself,

usan went back to her work, dreaming of being the next
maid to start working upstairs.

After she left, the duke went back to his desk, and
dumped out the contents of the velvet sack across his
mahogany writing-desk. He was horrified by what he saw.

There was a gold necklace of single square emeralds,
each one surrounded by an outline of diamonds, with
earrings and bracelet to match.

There was a necklace formed by a web of sparkling
diamond drops, with earrings and bracelet to match.

There was a necklace of rubies, with matching earrings.
There was a necklace, bracelet, and earrings of matched
pearls.

There was a fabulous diamond tiara.

Mary had obviously stolen someone's entire set of jewelry—or she had taken one piece from each house she
robbed. There was no help for it at all: the girl was bound
for the gallows.

Putting all the jewels back in the bag, he went across
and knocked on the door of his mother's sitting-room,
where the dowager was writing a letter to a friend. He
spread out the jewels over her working table.

"Mother, do you recognize these pieces? Do you know
to whom they may belong?"

"Very nice. Where did you find them?"

"In the possession of Mary," he said sternly.

"Then they belong to her, I suppose."

"What do you mean?"

"Haven't you seen her? I heard she was called down
to talk to you."

"I gave orders she be called to my sitting-room; there
were some visitors who called to see her on urgent business; they said she had stolen a ring of theirs. I was upset,
and I did not stay."

"Stolen a ring of theirs?" cried the dowager in alarm "Lady Mary?"

"Who is Lady Mary?"

"*Our* Mary is Lady Mary; she is the Lady Mary Hamilton of Danby Court, Cumberland—the daughter of the late Earl and Countess of Hamilton. I thought you knew by now. Once she revealed her true identity to me, thought she was on her way to inform you at once."

"I had already left the parlor."

"Charles, you do not mean to tell me you have left her alone with her stepfather, do you?"

"I'm afraid so."

"He has designs on her fortune—has been scheming to wrest control of the Hamilton estate by marrying of his nephew to her, and petitioning to recreate the earldom. They have successfully abducted her once already—that is why she fled to London, and why she decided to hide as a housemaid, until she can claim the estate in her own right at twenty-one. She must not be left alone with those men!"

"Calm yourself, Mother. This is my house—they can't abduct anyone from here, not in broad daylight."

"Go to her at once, Charles! You don't understand how much the poor child has suffered at their hands already!"

"Of course she has! I am so ashamed—ashamed of what I have said, and what I have thought, and how have acted. Mother, I have wronged that girl, and I have wronged her deeply. I fell in love with her the moment I saw her, but all along the way I misjudged her, and injured her. My god, Mother, what a fool I have been!"

"Yes, my dear," said his mother bluntly, "you have. Pray do not compound your error, Charles: find Lady Mary at once."

*   *   *

The duke swung open the door to the parlor so hard
hit the wall, and caused a vase to crash to the floor in
ieces. Mary was nowhere to be seen. The two gentlemen
ho had been there had disappeared, as well.

The duke swore mightily, and dashed down the stairs
the hall porter. Furious questioning quickly revealed
at the porter had seen a young person carried off
rapped in a shawl, and bundled into the gentlemen's
oach. He told the duke that the older man had reported
him that someone had been taken ill, and required
nmediate medical attention. The coach had driven off
high speed.

The duke swore once again, and called for his town-
oach. When it had been brought around, the coachman
sked for orders.

At that point he realized he had no idea where they
ight have gone with Lady Mary.

Chapter 28

The duke, in a blind fury, set out as soon as his hasty discussion with his mother revealed the exact direction of Hamilton House. His grace's town-coach, its horses all blowing, pulled up at a handsome mansion of excellent proportion and line.

The duke strode up some stairs, knocked soundly, and sought admission. The porter, who gave his grace a wary look, did not ask him to step inside the parlor, but closed the door and went within. In a few minutes he returned with the message that no one was at home to accept visitors.

"Step aside, man," said the duke, raising his fists in a threatening fashion. "I will not be denied."

The porter sized up the visitor as one who must have spent many hours at Gentleman Jackson's in order to be so confident, and, mindful of his desire not to serve as an unwitting sparring partner, he allowed his grace to pass.

"Now, tell me where they've taken the girl." The porter, with a guilty look, indicated upstairs, and the duke went up, two steps at a time.

He went into a large salon, where two men were standing, talking.

"And who may you be, my good man?" inquired Sir Barton with a sneer, turning to look at the intruder.

"I am Sarratt," he thundered.

Sir Barton's expression changed to one of fawning subservience, and he began gesturing toward one of the Hepplewhite chairs.

"You honor me with your presence, your grace," he said. "Do sit down. Pray send your mother my compliments—she was so helpful to us in such a difficult circumstance. Perhaps she may have explained things to you. We had a robbery of some precious family jewels, as we earlier explained. Thanks to your mother's intervention, it has all come right, however."

"Where is the Lady Mary Hamilton?" he roared, even louder than before. "Tell me at once what you have done with her!"

Sir Barton backed up several paces, and began wringing his hands.

"Ah, well, your grace. That is a long story, and best explained at length. Family matter. Bit of a scandal. Best not to mention it. Most improper girl."

The duke planted Sir Barton with a facer that dropped him full on the floor, and drew his cork.

The duke turned to Gervase, who was widely known in Dunberton as a great coward.

"Shall I repeat myself? Or will you tell me where the Lady Mary is?"

"No, no, your grace. There is no problem at all— I'll tell you. The girl is upstairs in her room, and quite unharmed. I am glad to see you are so concerned about her welfare."

"Obviously so."

"The thing is, man," Gervase said confidentially, "begging your pardon, what my uncle was about to say was, well, the gal's made rather a nasty scandal, that's the trouble. Posing as maid in your household? Not at all the thing, is it? The gal's just not behaved as she ought. My uncle and I couldn't let her ruin the name of Hamilton, could we? No, she could not be allowed to keep up that pretense a moment longer. We had to rush her out at once to put an end to the whole sad adventure.

"You understand, of course. Can't let one's name be bandied about, stories and speculations and all that sort of nasty thing. We were just tryin' to hush it up, keep things in the family. Know what I mean?

"We'll help the girl, don't you worry, your grace. I'm still willing to marry her, give her the protection of my name, try to put the best face on it. Whole thing will die down in time. Nothing for your grace to concern himself with."

At this piece of impertinence, his grace of Sarratt saw fit to knock Gervase down, too.

When, after a minute or so, the foolish man tried to stand up again, Sarratt gave him another blow, just out of ill-temper.

Once he had regained consciousness, the duke said to him, "Whatever concerns the Lady Mary Hamilton, concerns me. I intend to make that girl my wife; I intend that she bear my children. Is that perfectly clear to you?

"You—and your uncle—will generally retract any and all the tales you have ever told about Lady Mary Hamilton, until I am satisfied the world knows precisely who was at fault in these affairs.

"If I ever hear of you sullying her good name again, or anyone else's, I will make known to the proper authorities your fortune-hunting scheme, and thus cause you to

be clapped in prison and transported to Australia. Have
I made myself perfectly clear on that point, as well?"

"Yes, your grace," whined Gervase. "Please don'
strike me again."

"Remove yourself from my sight, worm, and bring m
the Lady Mary. No; don't do that; she won't want to cas
her eyes on your miserable countenance. I'll find he
myself. She is upstairs?"

"Yes, your grace. First room on the right. Take he
away, please. I don't want any more trouble; she's alread
caused me heaps of it."

He bounded up the steps again, two at a time, lookin
for Lady Mary. Finally, he opened a door and found he
lying on a large canopied bed, weeping.

"Mary!" he cried, throwing himself at her feet. "Wil
you ever forgive me? I've been such a fool!"

"You can't want me, your grace, not after everythin
that's happened," she said miserably.

"My name is Charles, and don't be a pea-goose. I hav
wanted you since the first moment I met you. I have love
you these many weeks.

"I am so sorry for all the things I said about you—
was mad with jealousy when I saw you in Roger Hench
art's arms. My intention, in wanting you to marry me
was not at fault, but I gave in to the passion of the momen
and would not let you defend yourself. That was wron
of me, and I beg you will grant me your pardon."

"I do not care about that—I was upset, then. We bot
were.

"The real problem, however, is not that, but my reputa
tion—all the rumors about me. My stepfather told m
that they have already spread stories about me all aroun
town. Everyone now thinks the worst of me: they thin
that I urged Gervase to abduct me, and that I cared nothin
about being ruined. They put it about that I'm a wil

hoyden who took employment as a maid on a lark. You can't not care about that: everyone will set up their backs against me. What will your mother think? What will Diana think? What will the world think?"

"As to my mother and Diana, they think you a perfect darling. As to what the world thinks, I don't care a fig about it. As to what my friends think, they will only envy me.

"If you will kindly do me the honor of consenting to marry me, I'll lend you the protection of my name and my credit. No one in the ton will dare to say anything against you: and, you will be my wife, her grace Mary, Duchess of Sarratt."

"I don't care about being a duchess," she offered after a moment of silence, in a shy, soft voice, "but I would very much like to be your wife."

"Would you?" he asked, bending down to kiss her.

"I would, your grace. Let me show you what I mean," said Lady Mary, who then showed him very precisely.

Chapter 29

"It's just a bit ancient, isn't it, Charles?" said the Duchess of Sarratt, using her hand to brush off the long scarlet robe trimmed with the requisite four rows of ermine.

"Yes, certainly," admitted the duke. "It's been a long stretch between coronations. On the other hand, one does not really want to be forced to order a new set made with every new generation."

"Certainly not," chimed in the dowager. "That would be most imprudent. Being so amazingly dear, coronation robes should suffice for two or three generations at the least. These will do very well for now, with a little attention."

The Marquess of Allingham, half-dressed in nankeen, crawled with remarkable alacrity through the parlor at this point, followed close behind by Fanny Simpson, who was in charge of him, followed by Susan Bowker, his fond nursery maid, who was carrying the remainder of his lordship's clothes.

"Beg pardon, your grace," said Susan. "Lord Allingham has so much gumption today I can hardly keep up with him. I don't know how he does it; he's still so little. This is the second time he's gotten the best of me and escaped the nursery."

"Do the best you can with him," said his lordship's mother with a sigh.

"How we shall ever find a tutor to control that child when he's grown up, I don't know," said the dowager. "That boy has been irrepressibly spirited since birth, and he's not yet out of leading-strings."

"Takes after his mother, Mother," said the duke.

The duchess gave her husband a severe look, and returned to her work. Farley, who wished the quality would leave this sort of thing entirely to the staff, removed her grace's coronet from its case; the duchess brushed off the top of it, and blew the dust off the strawberry leaves.

"I must say, this looks to be rather a fun thing to wear."

"It isn't. A bit awkward, really.

"Lady Adelaide Henchart always had her eye on that coronet, did I ever mention that?" said the dowager. "Did you know that when she used to visit me, she nagged and nagged at me to show her the thing. I grew so tired of it that I actually gave in, and had them brought down to show her. The Sarratt jewels, too. I promise you, when she set her eyes on them, her mouth fairly watered. I'd never seen such a thing in my life. So vulgar."

"Poor Adelaide," said the duchess. "It's so awfully sad what happened to her."

"Indeed. To be forced to become a paid companion."

"And not 'paid' very much."

"It must be such a sore trial to her, as she always had been so very high in the instep!"

"And to be a companion to Lady Witherspoon—a

orrid old cat if ever there was one. You really can't have
worse luck than that," said the duke.

"I'm surprised she could not find *some* eligible person
ɔ marry her."

"After that scandal with Lord Rutherfurd, and Roger?
The entirety of their estates wagered away in six weeks'
mad gambling? The only heir learning of their losses,
and taking his own life? Who would marry into such a
scandal?"

"Well, dear, after all—*you* married into scandal," the
duchess reminded the duke.

"Your scandal was insignificant," said the duke. "It
didn't last around town above a day, once the character
f your stepfather became generally known. Besides, you
were worth every bit of it."

"Thank you, my love, for your continuing confidence
ı me."

"Will you two stop billing and cooing long enough to
ecide whether these robes will do? I'm sure that Farley
and Boswell wish to take them away and get on with
hings."

Thomas entered, and handed a note on a silver salver
ɔ the duchess.

She broke the wafer and scanned the contents.

"Oh, dear," she said. "It's from Diana. Little Lady
Caroline has the croup, so Diana and Weymouth won't
e coming to dine tonight."

"I hope young Charles won't catch it," said the dowa-
er in an anxious tone. "You know how these things can
ɔ round town. Think of Townsend's children—they lost
wo of them to the measles, in no time at all."

"Don't worry, Mother. He won't fall ill. He's really
ery resilient," said his proud father.

"But what if he's not? One must be prepared for all
ventualities, even tragic ones. Really, Charles: you have

a duty to your lineage. You really *must* have more children Charles, you know.''

''More children? Why, Mother!'' said the duke, with a distinct sparkle in his eyes, bringing to his wife's lovely face the deepest possible blush, ''What an excellent suggestion!''